SAVANNAH'S CURSE

SAVANNAH'S CURSE

Shelia M. Goss

URBAN
Renaissance

www.urbanbooks.net

Urban Books, LLC
78 East Industry Court
Deer Park, NY 11729

ISBN 13: 978-1-60162-247-1
ISBN 10: 1-60162-247-3

First Trade Paperback Printing March 2011
Printed in the United States of America

10 9 8 7 6 5 4 3 2 1

Distributed by Kensington Publishing Corp.
Submit Wholesale Orders to:
Kensington Publishing Corp.
C/O Penguin Group (USA) Inc.
Attention: Order Processing
405 Murray Hill Parkway
East Rutherford, NJ 07073-2316
Phone: 1-800-526-0275
Fax: 1-800-227-9604

SAVANNAH'S CURSE

A NOVEL

BY

SHELIA M. GOSS

Dedication

This is dedicated to all the men and women in the armed forces who are keeping us safe. I would also like to dedicate this book in memory of my father, Lloyd Goss, and grandfather, JC Hogan.

Prologue

Dreams are like the doorway to one's reality.

Savannah Blake shouted, "Daddy," right before waking up from the nightmare she would not remember. She glanced at the clock; it was a few minutes after nine. She couldn't believe she overslept—if sleep was what it was really called. Savannah had plans on meeting her father for breakfast to discuss an idea about her new business venture. Unlike the old ones, this idea would be right up his alley. This one was to own and run a project-management consulting firm. With her father's keen sense of business, Savannah couldn't fathom making a decision without his approval, and she was certain she'd have it this time.

Savannah took a shower, and while the water slid down her body, she thought about her mother. Her father never let her forget that she was the spitting image of her. Ellen Danielle Blake—that was her mother's name. Both of them were petite and chose to wear their jet-black hair long and wavy. Ellen had died a few months after giving birth to Savannah's youngest sister, Asia. The bittersweet memory of losing her mother when Savannah was only age six still stung. Savannah wiped away the lone tear that fell from one eye. Her father raised them in Louisiana until his job re-assigned him to an office in Texas. Savannah and her sisters lived in Texas, but their father never let them forget their Louisiana heritage.

As she dried off, she glanced at the clock. "Sheesh, where does the time go?" she asked rhetorically, seeing that she was late. Being punctual was something her dad had instilled in them all. Her sisters, Montana and Asia, would tease her if they knew she was late. She prepared herself for a lecture from her dad.

Savannah dialed her father's number while exiting her town house, taking brisk and wide strides. "That's odd," she said as she called his cell phone, just in case he was outside working in the garden. Her father never went anywhere without his cell phone.

Arriving at her father's house a short time later, she pulled out the spare key, without a thought to ringing the bell. "Sorry, I'm late," she shouted, entering the house, instantly taking in the aroma of fresh brewed coffee and bacon and eggs, which filled every inch of the air. Cooking was just one of many talents her father possessed.

"Daddy, where are you?" Savannah shouted again, when she didn't see him in the kitchen or dining room. Only then did she notice that the patio door was ajar.

Expecting to find her father outside tending to his geraniums, she stepped over the threshold and onto the brick deck, the same deck she and her sisters had helped him lay.

As if a flash of bright light had taken her vision, she was blinded by the view ahead. She screamed at both the instant surprise and the sight that lay before her. Her father lay sprawled out on the ground. It was as if a camera flashed, leaving behind a portrait that would forever hang on her mental walls.

"Daddy! Daddy!" she shouted.

The words, the sound of her own voice at that pitch, caused her head and ears to ache and her brain to delay its registration of data.

The mental delay continued. Blood seeped through the brown multi-striped shirt he was wearing. She knelt down next to his body.

"My father. . . ," she slurred the words out loud, hoping to rush the process along. "My father has been shot," she panted, dipping her shaking hands into her pocket for her cell phone. Her heartbeat increased to a rapid pace. "My father. . . ," she said, grasping for control of her voice, turning her head away from his body while dialing 911. She glanced back, "Oh God!" she squealed as the operator came on.

"911," the operator said, sounding controlled and emotionally well managed.

Savannah shouted the ill-rehearsed lines her brain had just at that second computed. "My father's been shot! Oh my God!" she screamed.

"Ma'am, we need you to calm down," the operator said, still sounding fully controlled.

The conflict of the woman's calm voice versus the scene that lay before her tightened Savannah's stomach, or maybe it was her brain's fault that she was feeling instantly sick. For now, her brain was bringing in the moment full force—the sounds of the flies buzzing in the Texas heat, the smells of the coagulating blood on the bricks, the water pouring out of the water hose.

"What's the address?" the woman asked.

Holding her face, Savannah felt the moisture on her hands. "Oh God, his blood is on my hands," she gasped, giving way to hysterical tears.

"The address?" the woman repeated.

In between the tears Savannah managed to stammer out her father's house number and street. "There's blood everywhere," Savannah added, looking at her blood-covered hands. "I think I touched him. I must have touched him."

"It's okay, ma'am. Just stay calm. Now I need to know if he's conscious."

"Conscious?" she asked. She saw her father's eyes flutter. "Yes, but. . . ," Savannah's voice trailed. "You have to come . . . now!" Panic set in instantly as she hung up the phone and again gave her attention to her father. This time she was conscious of her actions. She knew what she was saying and doing.

"Daddy," Savannah whimpered as her hands hovered over him. She pondered if she should move him, or if she could help him somehow. Finally she gave up in her attempt to reason and scooped him up in her arms. "Daddy. . . ," she cried.

"Baby girl," he whispered, choking on the blood that was no doubt forming in his throat.

"Shh," Savannah said as she held him and rocked him the way he used to rock her on so many scary nights when she was a child. Sleep had never been her friend, and so all she could figure was that he would fight this last good-bye. Tears soaked her face, and now his.

"The box is in the attic. . . The key . . . go to bank . . . safe-deposit," he whispered.

"Wha-what?" Savannah asked, figuring he was delusional, or her ears were playing tricks on her. How could he be thinking about a key and a box when his life was in jeopardy? "I love you, Daddy. . . They are coming, and things are going to be all right. You don't have to go to sleep. Stay awake with me," Savannah said, refusing to give in to anything negative. He had to be all right. Her mind couldn't grasp being without him, her only parent. Again her stomach tightened as the sound of the sirens filled her ears.

He managed to spit out, in between coughing up blood, "I love you."

"Daddy. . . ," she squealed, squeezing a stream of fresh hot tears from her squinted eyes.

"Your sisters . . . Contact Bridges. He'll know what to do for your sisters. . ."

"Just hold on, Daddy. I hear them coming," Savannah begged. She wanted to show him she was strong, and he was going to be all right. But she knew this time her façade of strength would not hold. Her performance as a pillar of fortitude was a flop.

Her dad shifted in her arms, and suddenly, as if full of clarity, as if moving from this life into the next one—a happier one—in a clear crisp voice, he said, "I love you."

The floodgate of tears opened. "Daddy . . . Dad, I—"

"Shh, sweetheart." He paused, then attempted to raise his hand to touch her but dropped it listlessly to the ground. "I'm proud of you. You're stronger than what you think you are." He appeared to be looking past Savannah into the distance. It was so definite a gaze that she, too, looked over her own shoulder. Looking back, she caught his eyes closing.

"No, Daddy, stay with me. Please don't do this." Savannah rocked him back and forth, holding him close, not concerned about his blood covering her shirt.

"Don't cry, baby. Everything is going to be all right," he mumbled.

Tears streamed down her face. "Not without you."

Silence caused her to release her tight grip and look at her father's face again. She had to know if he was still alive. He had to be alive!

"Savannah, promise me you'll protect your sisters," he said before his eyes closed. This time it was for good.

She envisioned Major Blake, her father, rising from the ground and stepping through death's door. Gone was the bloodstained shirt that adorned his earthly body; a long white robe now replaced it.

With Savannah holding his body with one arm, and raising her hand to wave at him with the other, she gave in to the momentary out-of-body experience she found herself in. "Good-bye," he said, smiling at her before following a tall, handsome man standing beside him. The scene disappeared into the portal of her mind's eye. She glanced back at the body in her arms.

All her senses were on alert. "Daddy?" she called.

The door opened as the paramedics burst onto the deck. They were late. They were a moment too late.

Some came through the house, some through the back gate—late, all the same.

She could tell people were surrounding the house. That's when she noticed the Dallas police officers' uniforms, in addition to the firemen's and paramedics'. So many uniforms of different types were there. Her eyes fluttered, but she held on to the moment. This was not a time to give in to the mental overload.

With tears streaming down her face, Savannah kissed her father on his forehead for the last time before those men, with forcefulness and tactless hands, shoved her out of the way. "Excuse me, miss," one said, noticing her falling back onto the deck with a thud.

As she watched them work, she could only think of their poor timing. They were seconds too late to save the one man in her life who never disappointed her, and who meant the world to her. Major Blake died in her arms, but his legacy would live on.

Soon they, too, would want to know the answers to what she already questioned. Who had killed her father?

But what they didn't know was that Savannah had made a vow—whoever it was, they would not go unpunished.

~ 1 ~

Six months later . . .

"Happ—py birthday to youuuu and many moooore," sang Montana and Asia. They blew on the party horns and threw the confetti in the air. It fell everywhere, messing up Savannah's recently styled Shirley Temple–curled hair.

Savannah shook some of the confetti off the top of her head before leaning over the purple rose-trimmed flat sheet cake and blowing out the flames above the 3 and 0. Normally, she wouldn't mind partying, but this year she didn't feel like celebrating. She faked a smile and tried to join in the fun. She didn't want her sisters to know how her heart ached not seeing their father standing beside them.

After the funeral Savannah had decided to sell her town house and moved back into their family home. At first it was hard, because her mind kept playing, over and over, the scene of finding her father. Montana tried to convince her to sell, but she wasn't having it. She agreed to buy them out of their share, but neither Montana nor Asia would accept her money. Savannah put her plans of starting her own project-management consulting firm on hold and took a sabbatical from her highly paid six-figure job. She had money saved, so, thanks to smart investments and her share of her father's life insurance policy, money was not an issue.

Savannah felt like the detectives handling her father's murder were incompetent. They were no closer to finding her father's killer than they were six months ago. She decided to get out of her depressed state and take action. In order for her to move on with her life, she needed closure, and the only way to do that was to find out who had murdered her father. Her task now was convincing her sisters to join her on the quest. Finding the right time to bring it up filled her mind as her sisters showered her with birthday greetings.

Asia, wearing a short blue jean mini-dress, handed her a gift bag. "I hope you like it."

Savannah pulled the purple tissue paper out and smiled when she pulled out a box collection of her favorite singer's CDs. Nothing cheered her up more than listening to songs by Aretha Franklin. Aretha Franklin's music reminded her of their mother. Her mother would always sing Aretha tunes around the house.

"Thank you, sis," she said as she hugged her.

Montana cleared her throat. Not wanting to be left out, she handed over, with her perfect manicured nails, a huge box with a red velvet bow around it.

Without hesitating, Savannah removed the bow. "Thanks for the foot spa tub. I could really use it." Savannah hoped she sounded convincing.

"Don't be jealous that my gift is more sentimental," Asia said.

"Whatever." Montana held up her hand in a "talk to the hand" gesture.

Some things never changed. Ever since they were little, Montana and Asia were competitive. With a two-year age difference between the two, they fought for Savannah's attention, their father's, and whoever else would give them the time of day. Their father never dissuaded them, because he thought it would help prepare them for the real world. Although Montana was now twenty-seven, and Asia was twenty-five, to watch them spar could be comical yet irritating. Savannah didn't think they even realized how ridiculous they looked.

Savannah looped an arm through each one of her sisters as they walked to the living room. "Let's do karaoke."

They spent the next hour singing to Aretha Franklin tunes, dancing and laughing. Savannah didn't want to end her birthday on a sour note, but she had a plan to avenge their father's death, and she would need their help.

"I have a few leads on who killed Daddy," Savannah said as they were almost through cleaning up the kitchen.

Montana and Asia looked at one another. Neither said a word. Montana wiped the same clean spot on the stove over and over. Asia washed the remainder of the dishes. The quiet was deafening.

"You are becoming obsessed with this." Montana waved the dish towel back and forth.

"He was our dad too, but, Savannah, you have to let this go," Asia added.

Savannah didn't respond.

Montana broke the silence. "What? What do you want from us? I'll do anything to wipe that pathetic look off your face."

"That's what I wanted to hear. Can you both come over tomorrow after you get off work? I have some things we need to discuss."

Montana crossed her arms. "I'm not going anywhere until you tell us everything now."

Asia's cell phone rang. She looked at the display and opted not to answer. "He can wait."

"Another one of your flunkies," Montana comment-ed.

"At least I have someone," she responded.

"Enough already!" Savannah screamed.

"Sorry," Montana mumbled.

Savannah pulled a box out from under a kitchen cabinet. They followed her to the kitchen table as Savannah removed several papers and pictures. She handed each one of her sisters copies of some of her notes. "We need to find out who killed dad."

"We?" Asia asked.

"Yes, us. I can't do this by myself. Dad taught each one of us special skills, and although we all have chosen other careers, I think it's time that we put those skills to use."

Montana ran her hand through her short-cropped hair. "Why don't we just hire someone?"

"To do what? Tell him if he finds the killer, we want him killed. I'm not trying to spend a day behind bars," Asia snapped.

"Both of you need to chill out. No one's going to jail." Savannah looked at Montana. "And we're going to find the killer ourselves."

Montana still didn't sound convinced. "Let's take a vote," she said.

"No need. I'm with Savannah. Dad would do the same for us," Asia responded.

"Should have known you would side with her," Montana mumbled.

Savannah ignored her. "Now that it's settled, I've printed out duplicate copies of information that you'll need to know." She handed them each some papers containing her notes on possible suspects. "Don't let this out of your sight. Review them and meet me back here tomorrow night."

Savannah watched them as they scanned the papers. She normally wouldn't put them in this situation, but there was no way she could live with herself if she didn't exhaust all avenues to locate their father's killer. "Dad was our protector, but some people might not like us digging into his murder. We need to take some precautions."

"What's this?" Montana asked as Savannah went to hand her a .38 Special, fully loaded.

Asia took her gun and inspected it. "I know you haven't forgotten how to shoot. 'Ms. think she can shoot better than me,'" Asia stated.

Savannah ignored Asia. "This is from Dad's collection. I know you don't like guns, but with everything that has happened, I think it's best."

Reluctantly Montana took the weapon and placed it in her purse.

A short time later, Savannah watched from the living-room window as her sisters entered their cars and left to go home. Due to it being quiet in the house, Savannah's body jerked at the sounds of the floor creaking near her. She didn't have any pets, so the creak had to mean one thing—an intruder had invaded her space. She could see someone in her peripheral vision. Savannah's natural instinct kicked in. With a quick, effortless spin around, she used some of her martial arts skills and ducked and did a sly kick, causing her surprise guest to fumble. With another move she had the culprit on the floor. She straddled his back, holding both of his arms. If she moved his left arm a few more inches, it would snap.

"Wait. I'm here to help," the somewhat-familiar voice of the strange man said between clenched teeth.

"Who are you?" Savannah asked.

"Let me up and I'll tell you."

Savannah tightened her grip. "Wrong answer."

"Ouch. I'm Bridges."

"Name doesn't sound familiar."

"I'm a friend of your father's."

Savannah wasn't sure if she could trust him. His words made her recall her father mentioning the name Bridges on his dying breath. She used her free hand and scratched the back of her head.

"I don't mean to sound like I'm complaining, but you have a mean grip on my arm, and it's hurting," the man said.

Savannah's surprise guest's voice did sound familiar. He also wore a familiar scent. It reminded her of the cologne her ex-boyfriend wore—Unforgivable. Bridges sneaking into her house uninvited was unforgivable. The urge to run her hands over his smooth, bald brown head left as quickly as it had come. She shook her head. What was she thinking? This man could be working with the man who killed her dad. She released both arms and moved her 150-pound frame from the top of his back.

As he stood up, she got a good look at the guy who called himself Bridges. His muscular build was no match for a woman who was trained to take men down three times her size. His cream-colored shirt and khaki pants were a little wrinkled from the attack. Bridges really did look so much like her ex-boyfriend. Savannah had to blink twice to make sure he wasn't a mirage—a strange figment of her imagination.

He moved his arms forward, rubbing both of them. "Thanks."

Savannah reached into the drawer of the table behind her without taking her eyes off him. He looked surprised to see her point a Glock at him. "You have five minutes and then I'm calling the cops."

"Four minutes." Something about his eyes was familiar to Savannah.

He reached for his pocket. Savannah clicked back the Glock. The sound stopped him. "I need to show you this e-mail I got from Major. From your dad."

Savannah patted her foot. "Go ahead, but I must warn you. If I see anything shiny, I'm shooting first and asking questions later."

Bridges removed his black wallet and took out a folded sheet of paper. He hesitantly walked closer to her, and was about to hand it to her, when Savannah said, "Hold it up."

He did as instructed. Her eyes scanned the piece of paper. He could have forged the e-mail; but for now, she would pretend to trust him. That is, until she could find out more about who this Bridges guy was, and how he knew her dad. A little relief swept through her body as she lowered her gun, but she refused to take her hand off the trigger.

"Have a seat," she said as she motioned for him to move forward toward the living room. "Excuse the paper. My sisters and I were celebrating. Well, anyway, it doesn't matter. Just tell me how you knew my father."

"Savannah, it's me."

Savannah stared at him with a blank expression.

He continued, "It's me . . . Troy."

Savannah blinked her eyes a few times. So many questions ran through her mind. She always imagined what she would say or do if she ever saw Troy again. In her fantasies she would make love to him first, and then curse him out later. Now that he was actually sitting here in the flesh, Savannah was speechless. Her mind flashed back ten years. Ten years ago, she was a starry-eyed college student head over heels in love with Troy Nelson, not Troy Bridges. Regardless of what name he was using now, Troy left her heartbroken, and for that, she should aim the gun and shoot him in the heart. Fortunately for him, she loved her freedom too much.

Troy didn't expect to be manhandled by the beauty, who stood five feet six inches tall. When he approached the house, he had heard Savannah and her sisters; he wanted to catch her by herself. From what Major had told him, Savannah and his other daughters were more than capable of taking care of themselves. His task now was to convince Savannah that she needed him as much as he needed her. She had some key information somewhere in this house, and he decided to go about it the right way. With his training, Troy could have done a sweep of the house, and, most likely, she never would have known he was there. But then again, if memory served him correctly, Savannah was a stickler for things being out of place and would have noticed if one item had been moved. He hadn't counted on his old feelings for Savannah to resurface so soon. There was barely a day that went by that Troy didn't think about her.

Troy had kept up to date via Savannah's father on the comings and goings of her life. She was definitely a knockout, literally and figuratively speaking. He wished he could have met her under normal circumstances. Troy recalled the few months of peace and joy Savannah had brought to his life ten years ago. She had a way of making him feel good, in and out of the bedroom. The look she gave him now was a far cry from how she used to look at him. If looks could kill, he would be six feet under.

"I don't have all night," Savannah said as she stared at him with her piercing ebony eyes.

Troy contemplated how much he wanted to reveal to Savannah. He decided to go the honest approach; well, as honest as he could be in the line of work he was accustomed to.

"Major was my lead operative. He was who I reported to while out in the field." Troy held back his emotions. He didn't want Savannah to see how much seeing her in person affected him. Major's loss hurt him too. Major understood him and always had his back when he would go about handling cases in nontraditional ways. Major was the one who encouraged him to start his own private-security firm.

Savannah watched with curiosity. She sensed something besides a boss/colleague affiliation. She could tell Troy had more of a personal relationship with her father, and she wanted to know how personal.

"My dad never talked about you." Savannah couldn't help but wonder how Troy and her dad's paths crossed. She met Troy while attending college and no one knew about their love affair, or so she thought. How did Troy end up working for SNA, the Securities National Agency known more commonly as "The Agency"?

"It was standard that we were not to discuss our business affairs with our family. That way, if any assignment went awry, the less our families knew, the safer they would be."

Savannah crossed her arms and leaned back in her chair. "That's why I hate secrets now."

"Your dad loved you all. He always talked about you."

"That's odd, because I can't recall ever hearing him speak of you, or hardly anyone else for that matter from work. The only person I know of is Uncle Raymond." The sparkle in Savannah's eyes disappeared.

Troy was tempted to reach over and comfort Savannah, but he knew any movement from him could result in him being back down on the floor. This time however he would be prepared. A sly grin formed at the thought.

"Your dad thought it would be best if he didn't talk about our missions with you and your sisters. The less you knew, the safer you would be. Well, that's what he thought, anyway," Troy stated.

"How do I know you're telling me the truth?"

"You'll have to trust me."

Savannah grunted. "Try again."

Troy shifted in his seat. "Your uncle Raymond is my ex-boss. You can call him and confirm, if you like."

"I just might do that."

Savannah pressed a button on her cell phone. The phone beeped to indicate it was on speaker. He watched her dial ten digits without once taking her eyes off him. They both listened to the high-pitched rings.

"Baby girl, how are you?" Uncle Raymond asked.

"I'm fine. I was going through Dad's stuff and had a few questions."

There was silence on the other end. Savannah was the first to speak. "Uncle Raymond, you're there?"

"Yes, dear. I was in the middle of something. Can I call you back?" he asked.

"It'll only take a few minutes. I promise."

"Okay. Well, hurry it up now."

"What do you know about Bridges? Troy Bridges?"

"Bridges? Why do you ask?"

"I told you I ran across some information of my dad's." Savannah became fidgety in her seat. She hated when she wasn't able to get a direct answer.

"He's no longer with The Agency, and that's all I can say."

"Thanks, Uncle."

"Savannah?"

"Yes."

"Stay clear of Troy. He's trouble with a capital *T*. I could never keep a rein on him when he was with us. Your dad was the only one who could tame him."

"Don't worry. I don't plan on having anything to do with him."

"That's a relief."

Savannah didn't know how to respond to that statement. She felt embarrassed because Troy Bridges, or whatever name he went by now, was sitting there listening to the entire conversation.

"I'll let you get back to whatever you were doing."

"Before you go, answer this. Did you find any other papers of your dad's?"

Savannah was about to answer when Troy shook his head back and forth. Savannah didn't know why she trusted the guy, but instead of telling Uncle Raymond the truth, she responded, "No. It was just a card with this Bridges guy's name on it, and I don't recall meeting him at the funeral. That's all. No big deal."

"Well, if you or your sisters need anything, and I do mean *anything,* don't hesitate to give your old uncle Raymond a call now."

"I won't," Savannah said before discontinuing the call.

Savannah turned and looked at Troy. "I don't know why I lied to him, but you better hope I don't live to regret it."

"You lying to him had nothing to do with me. Apparently, he doesn't know your plans."

"What plans?" Savannah asked innocently.

"What I'm about to say will either make you shoot me or hit me, but I'm prepared for both."

Savannah's eyes darkened. "Spill it."

"I know you're looking for your dad's killer. The Agency has had you under surveillance since your dad died. I'm not sure of what your dad told you, but the Securities National Agency is an organization that only a few select people in the government know exist. The main purpose of the organization is to eliminate any threats to our national security on our own soil and abroad."

Savannah placed her hand on her weapon. "I hope there's more to why you're here."

Troy never took his eyes off Savannah's hands. "I know you're eager to aim that at me."

"You're right." Savannah held up the gun. "I should shoot you right now, but I don't know how I would justify killing you."

"You could always say you killed an assailant." Troy was toying with her.

She held the gun down and placed it on her thigh, without removing her hand. "So you knew my dad. So you worked for The Agency. It still doesn't explain why you're here." And under her breath she said, "And why you left me ten years ago."

"Major suspected that some of the agents we worked with were shady. Since I now work independently, he felt he could trust me to get to the bottom of it. The only thing is, someone else must have known your dad was onto something and had him killed."

"Dad was retired. How and why did this happen now?" The tears formed before Savannah could control it.

Troy forgot all about the gun Savannah had on her thigh. If she shot him, so be it. He didn't hesitate to get up out of his seat and rush over to comfort her. He placed his arms around her. Reluctantly, she leaned on his shoulder and cried until she couldn't cry anymore.

"Let it all out. I cared about your dad too," Troy said. "That's why I've made it my duty to find out who did it . . . even if it's the last case I handle."

Savannah felt strength in his words. She removed herself from his embrace. He handed her a tissue off the table. She blew her nose. She felt embarrassed for her show of emotions but didn't know how to express herself. Memories of her father and seeing Troy after all these years overwhelmed her. She stood up and walked over to the mantel. She picked up picture after picture, pictures of her dad with her mom, pictures of her dad with her and each one of her sisters.

"This has been an emotional day: my birthday, my dad not being here, seeing you again. And now you're saying someone at The Agency, where my dad committed the majority of his life, might be responsible for his death. It's just surreal."

Troy knew his time for comforting Savannah had passed. He allowed her the space she needed to gain her composure.

Savannah pushed her pride aside and turned around and looked Troy straight in the eyes. "I'm prepared to pay you whatever amount you want. But I need your help to find my daddy's killer."

Troy didn't blink. "This one is on the house."

~ 3 ~

"Let's start over," Troy suggested. "I'm Troy Bridges, a friend and an ex-colleague of Major Blake's."

He extended his hand out toward Savannah.

Savannah looked at it for a second before reaching to shake it. "I'm Savannah. Well, you know that. This is silly."

They both laughed. "If you want a slice of cake, there's plenty left over," Savannah suggested.

"I'll take a piece, if you promise it's not laced with arsenic," Troy said.

Savannah winked, and a wicked smile adorned her face. "You'll just have to try it and find out."

Moments later, Savannah returned with a huge slice of cake with purple icing and a can of ice-cold soda. Savannah watched the man who came into her life like a whirlwind. With the information he shared about a traitor at the agency, Savannah knew she and maybe even her sisters were in danger. This made it even more imperative to find out who had killed her dad. She had vowed not to involve her uncle Raymond, and now she wasn't so sure. Maybe with his connections he could confirm or disprove Troy's allegations. If her father thought someone was a traitor, the proof was somewhere. The question was where. Maybe Troy knew more than what he was telling her. For now, she would have to trust him enough to get the information she needed. She hoped it wouldn't be the second time in her life that he abused her trust.

Troy's voice broke her train of thought. "That was good."

She watched him wipe the crumbs from around his sexy mouth. His lips reminded her of the rapper LL Cool J. "I know you said you were looking for information to help find my father's killer, but you could have done that without my help. What did you really come here for?" Savannah blurted out.

"I was wondering when you were going to get to that." Savannah looked at her watch. "I've wasted time. Can't afford to waste any more."

"Touché," Troy responded.

Savannah crossed her legs and waited for Troy's response.

"One of the last communications between Major and me was about a safe-deposit box. He said that if he died, you were the key."

Troy's response was not exactly the response she was looking for. She was speaking of something more personal. She wanted to know why he had left her. She still remembered the countless number of e-mails and phone calls going unanswered. She remembered going by his apartment and learning from his neighbor he had moved without a forwarding address. The day she learned that was the day her heart grew cold. No man had ever been able to get close to her since. She pushed her personal feelings aside and concentrated on his only purpose for being here—solving her father's murder.

Savannah had a revelation. "That's what he meant about a key."

"So you do know what I'm talking about?" Troy asked.

"Sort of. I haven't gone to the safe-deposit box yet." Savannah looked away. "I know what you're thinking.

I should have done it months ago. I just started going through the stuff in my dad's personal box."

"Can I see it?" Troy asked.

"Wait right here."

When Savannah returned with the wooden box, Troy's back was turned, but she could hear him talking to someone on his cell phone. "I'll be there shortly."

Savannah figured it was probably his wife or girlfriend. A chill went up her spine as she recalled the last time they made love. It was the same night she confessed her love for him, and the last night she saw him. He was a thing of her past. So what if he was married or had a girlfriend? How they dealt with his commanding personality—well, she didn't know, but it was their problem, not hers.

"You can come closer. I felt your presence the moment you walked back in the room," Troy said before turning around.

"My dad used to say the same thing."

"Something you pick up over the years," Troy responded. He sat on the couch. Instead of sitting across from him as she previously had, she made a point of sitting in the spot right next to him on the couch.

Savannah removed the papers out of the box and handed them to Troy. "This is what I've discovered so far."

He scanned each page. Savannah watched how his brow would rise or fall with each piece of paper he read.

"This is a lot of information. Who else knows about this?" Troy asked.

"Just you and me," she lied. Until she knew more about the new Troy, she didn't want him to know how much her sisters knew.

"Good. Let's keep it that way."

"I have a few questions for you."

"I'll try to answer."

"I realized after you disappeared on me that there was a lot about you that I didn't know. You never talked about your family. I didn't even know if you had a sister or a brother."

Troy, ashamed, looked away. "I'm sorry."

"Sometimes sorry isn't enough. For now, all I want to know is why are you doing this?"

"Your dad was more than my immediate supervisor. He was like a father figure to me. My own dad died when I was very young, so my mother had to raise my sister and me by herself. They both were killed in a train accident when I was sixteen."

Savannah wanted to reach out and comfort him by touching his face, but she didn't. Instead, she held on to the piece of paper she was holding tighter. "Sorry to hear that. Why didn't you tell me this when we met?"

Troy had a faraway look in his eyes. "I stayed at friends' houses, until one of the parents let my coach know. See, I was on the basketball team, and Coach Nelson . . . Well, he was the best. He convinced his wife to let me stay with them. I stayed with them until I graduated from high school and would return to visit them in between breaks while in college."

"That was nice of them."

"Yes, it was. I don't know where I would have ended up if they hadn't."

"Where are they now?"

Savannah saw what looked to be tears forming in Troy's eyes. "Someone murdered them. Someone broke in and brutally murdered them. I can remember the day like it was yesterday. After I finished my last class, I caught a Greyhound bus home to visit them. They were supposed to meet me at the bus station. I waited and waited. When they didn't show up at the bus station, I hitched a ride home—"

"You don't have to," Savannah interrupted. She could feel the pain resonating in his voice.

He wiped his eyes with the back of his hands. "I never returned to college. I needed to get far away from everything. I joined the army and I got recruited for Special Forces. That's where I met your dad. He could tell I was dealing with some issues. He helped me work through them."

"Dad was always good at reading people." Savannah smiled as she reminisced about her dad. She frowned when she asked the next question. "Why didn't you tell me? It only took a phone call. I would have understood."

"I didn't even understand, so I didn't expect you to."

"But you left me. Left me thinking you had used me. Slept with me. Made me confess my love for you, and you threw it all away. We had plans. I was going to tell my family about you. About us." Savannah could not hold back the tears.

"Please don't cry, Vanna." Troy used her nickname.

"I haven't trusted a man since," Savannah confessed.

"When everybody I ever cared about ended up dead, I couldn't do anything. I didn't want you to end up dead too. I've always regretted not returning to campus one last time to tell you good-bye. I felt like my life wasn't worth living. I didn't want you to see me like that."

"I would have been there for you. I loved you."

"I loved you too. Enough not to bring you into my drama. I would not have been good for you after that."

"But I should have been the one to decide that—not you. You took away my options."

"Leaving you was the only option," Troy responded.

Savannah wiped the tears from her eyes, cleared her throat. "Did they ever find out who killed them?"

"No, when the Nelsons were killed, I couldn't do anything. I can do something about your father's death, though. If it's the last thing I do, I will find out who did it, and they will pay."

Savannah mumbled, "Remind me to stay on your good side."

He smiled for the first time since they started the conversation. "I need to be telling you that, Ms. Jackie Chan."

Savannah reenacted a karate hand move. "Daddy didn't raise a weakling."

Troy put the papers on the coffee table. "I'm curious. Do you really know how to shoot a gun?"

"Dad told me never to pull out a gun, unless I'm prepared to use it."

"I take that as an affirmative."

"Correct."

"Let's hope you never have to fire it. But just in case you do, why don't you meet me tomorrow at the firing range so I can see what you got?" Troy wrote an address on a piece of paper and handed it to her.

Savannah glanced at it. "I'll be there around noon, if that's okay."

"It's a date."

"I don't know if your significant other would like that," Savannah replied.

Troy ignored her comment. "Well, it's getting late, and I don't want to be the cause of you being late for work."

"I'm a big girl. I can take care of myself," Savannah flirted back.

"That I'm sure of," Troy responded.

Savannah walked him to the door. "I didn't see your car outside earlier. Where did you park?"

"About a block away."

"I'm surprised one of the neighbors didn't report an abandoned car."

"Trust me. I know not to draw attention to myself."

"I see. Good night, Mr. Bridges."

"Good night, Ms. Savannah. Lock up."

They stared at each other briefly. Troy broke the trance and walked out, closing the door behind him. Savannah made sure each latch was in place before peeking out the window. Troy had disappeared into the night. She activated the alarm before climbing up the stairs. If she didn't know any better, she would have thought Troy was a figment of her imagination. The only thing that made him real was the lingering scent of his cologne.

~ 4 ~

"I need to see your license and registration," the uniformed officer said to Troy as the policeman hid his face underneath a big-brimmed blue hat. The officer glanced at the license. With his weapon drawn he stated, "Troy Bridges, I need you to step out of the car now. Slowly."

Troy, perturbed because he was running late, exited the car. He made sure he put his hands in the air.

"Please step over there." The officer pointed to his right.

Troy stopped in midstep when he recognized the voice. "Meeks, is that you?"

"In the flesh. Had you squirming, didn't I?" Meeks placed the gun in his holster and removed his hat.

"Man, if you weren't in that uniform, I would take you down right now." Troy hadn't seen his friend Meeks in a few years, but he still looked the same— same closely cropped short hair. They gave each other a brotherly hug and leaned on Troy's black SUV.

"How you've been?" Meeks asked.

"Business is good. What about you?"

"Now that I'm divorced, it's all good."

"It has been a long time."

Before they could finish the conversation, an emergency alert sounded on Meeks's radio. "I'm on the way."

Meeks handed Troy a business card. "Don't be a stranger."

"I won't." Troy entered his SUV as Meeks turned on his siren and sped away.

Troy didn't believe in coincidences. He and Meeks were in the army together, and after a short stint in the special unit, Meeks got out and they hadn't spoken to each other in years. Troy placed the card in his wallet. He made a mental note to contact him as soon as he could.

Savannah tossed and turned the entire night. Visions of her dad and Troy wouldn't let her rest. She woke up in a cold sweat. After showering, dressing, and drinking her morning cup of coffee, cream with two packages of sugar substitutes, Savannah felt rejuvenated.

The hair on the back of her neck stood up. After Troy's surprise visit Savannah's senses were on extra alert. She went from room to room to make sure all was secure. "I'm being paranoid," she said out loud.

As Savannah exited the two-car garage in her candy-apple-red Mustang, she saw a black sedan, with tinted windows, pull away. Seeing Mr. Jacobs, one of her elderly neighbors, with his navy blue robe tied tight around his waist, waving his arms up and down, captured her attention. She stopped at the end of her driveway and rolled her passenger-side window down.

"Dear, they thought you weren't at home," Mr. Jacobs said as he placed his head through the window.

"I was in the bathroom."

"They were dressed in black suits. One was tall and bald, and the other was a short, pudgy dude. The short one was doing most of the talking."

"Did they happen to say who they were?"

"Something about being your father's friends."

Under her breath she said, "I doubt that." Savannah didn't want to alarm Mr. Jacobs into a heart attack, but she needed to warn him. "I'm not sure who those guys were, so if you see them or anyone suspicious around here, don't come out. Lock your doors and call the police. Promise me."

Mr. Jacobs looked confused. "I might be old, but I can take care of myself. So don't worry about me. Besides, I watch *CSI* every week."

Savannah held back a chuckle as she imagined him trying to fight someone. "I'm sure you can handle yourself, Mr. Jacobs, but please promise me. You don't want me worrying about you, do you?"

"Well, since you put it like that, I guess I'll do what you asked."

After making sure Mr. Jacobs promised to call the police, Savannah pulled out of the driveway. She checked her rearview mirror, just in case there was another car on the street with intentions of following her. She didn't know who the men in black were, but Savannah knew she didn't want to find out anytime soon. She continued to drive and check her mirror to see if she was being tailed as she headed to her destination.

While she sat at the light, she reviewed the directions Troy had given her to the shooting range. Her cell phone played the "Respect" ring tone. Montana's name flashed across the screen. She clicked on the speakerphone.

"What's up, sis?" Savannah asked.

"I'm taking off early because we need to talk."

"Talk to me."

"I don't want to discuss it over the phone."

"I'm not sure when I'll be back home. I'm on my way to a shooting range now."

"See, that's the kind of stuff I'm talking about. You are not G.I. Jane, so you need to chill. In fact, when I hang up from you, I'm calling Uncle Raymond. Maybe he can talk some sense into you."

Savannah pulled into a parking spot next to a black SUV. "You will do no such thing. I got some information I need to share with you and Asia. But you have to promise me you won't involve Uncle Raymond. At least, not until you hear me out."

"Vanna, I don't know. I'm just worried. We already lost Dad. I don't know what I'll do if I lost you too." From the sniffled sound coming from the other end of the phone, Montana sounded like she was crying.

"Sis, trust me. That's all I ask. Trust me."

"I do. But—"

"No buts. Look, I'm running late. I'll call you when I leave here." Savannah didn't wait for Montana to respond. She turned her ringer off, and after getting a feel for her surroundings, she exited her car.

"She finally graces me with her presence," Troy said after he greeted her with a hug. Savannah didn't hug him back. She decided at that point not to mention the men in black.

"I'm only a few minutes late. But, technically, I was here on time. I had a phone call that delayed me from entering the facility."

"Were you on the debate team in school?"

"No."

"Well, you should have been. Come on, let's suit up," Troy said as he led her to the property his company used for target practice.

Troy was impressed with the accuracy of Savannah's shooting. After she completed a few drills, he was confident she was ready for a special maneuver course he had set up specifically for his employees. With each maneuver Savannah took out her target.

Savannah popped her collar and said, "Anything else?"

"Yes, but I don't think this is the time or the place." The look of desire in Troy's eyes made Savannah look away.

Savannah knew she was flirting with disaster. Besides, she didn't want to start something with a man whom she could never trust with her heart again. Messing with Troy wasn't an option. "Now that you're satisfied I can handle myself with a weapon, what's next?"

"Give me about five minutes. Follow me to my office."

Savannah glanced at her watch. She felt guilty putting Montana off to hang out with Troy. "I would, but I have something else I need to do. Maybe another time."

"My office isn't far from here."

"I can meet you there in the morning."

"You know what? It's probably best that you don't. I'll meet you at your home later."

"I don't think it's a good idea. My sisters will be over tonight."

"But they were there last night."

"And? Is there a law about how many times siblings can visit each other that I don't know about?"

"No need for an attitude. There are things we need to discuss. Things we didn't discuss last night."

Savannah needed closure to their past relationship. Troy owed her that. She responded, "When my sisters leave, I'll call you."

"Promise?"

"Promise. Unlike you, I don't break mine."

On her way home Savannah stopped at the grocery store to pick up a roast and a bag of potatoes. She wanted to make her sisters' favorite meal. She would have their undivided attention, provided they had full stomachs. Savannah wasn't sure if she was ready to reveal her past with Troy. It would be hard enough to convince them to work with him without throwing in that extra information.

Every few minutes she found herself checking her rearview mirror to see if someone was following her. Since Savannah's unexpected visitors this morning, she decided to take extra precautions. Once securely in the house, she activated the alarm.

Less than two hours later the aroma of the roast filled the air. She stopped stirring the butter in the mashed potatoes when she heard the front door open. Montana and Asia both had keys and barely rang the doorbell; however, she couldn't help but be a little on edge. Savannah yelled, "Anybody there?"

"Vanna, it's me," Asia shouted. Asia sashayed in the room, wearing a pair of black slacks and gold satin shirt showing her cleavage. Her short Halle Berry–styled haircut accented her high cheekbones.

"Girl, don't tell me you wore that blouse to work."

Asia patted her bare chest. "What's wrong with it?"

"Don't let me go there."

"You're just an old maid."

"Whatever. I just don't believe in showing all of my assets."

Asia ran her hands down her side. "If you got it like I do, why not flaunt it."

Montana came in on the tail end of Asia's statement. "You're so superficial."

"I love you too," Asia responded.

"Don't start, y'all. Asia, set the table. I need to talk to Montana for a minute."

Asia crossed her arms. "No secrets—remember?"

"The longer it takes for you to set the table, the longer it'll take for me to bring the food out."

Asia rubbed her stomach. "You better be glad I'm hungry."

Once Savannah was sure Asia was out of earshot, she asked, "You haven't talked to Uncle Raymond, have you?"

"I told you I wouldn't." Montana frowned. "For now, anyway."

"Just checking. Take this to the table and I'll be there in a minute."

The chatter over dinner consisted of Montana and Asia discussing their jobs. Savannah waited until after the dishes were in the dishwasher and the kitchen was cleaned before bringing up the topic they were all there to discuss.

Savannah sat in her favorite spot on the love seat, while Montana sat in the chair and Asia slid down and sat on the floor. Each sister held a notebook with her prospective notes.

"The Blake sisters' official meeting starts now," Savannah joked.

Montana sighed. Savannah addressed her. "Do you want to say something?"

"No."

Savannah ignored Montana's attitude. "I had a surprise visitor when you two left last night." She told them about her encounter with Troy. She purposely left out information about their past relationship.

"Why didn't you call the cops?" Montana asked.

"Because I had the situation under control," Savannah responded.

"He could have killed you," Asia added.

"Believe me, I had the upper hand." Savannah smiled as she recalled having Troy pinned down.

Savannah informed them about Troy's association with their dad. "He's working for himself now. We need him because he knows the ins and outs of The Agency. Otherwise, we wouldn't need him."

"I don't like this." Montana frowned.

Asia asked, "How much does he know?"

"He claims to know what Dad knew." Savannah paused. "One other thing, he doesn't know you two know everything. I want to keep it like that."

"If you don't trust him, why are you willing to work with him? For all you know he could be playing you. He could be the weak link in The Agency that's behind dad's killing," Montana stated.

"You must not have heard a word she said," Asia chimed in. "He's an ex–secret operative. We need him."

"At this point, I don't trust anyone but you two. But we need someone who knows how they operate in the inside, and Troy is the man." Savannah hoped she sounded convincing.

Asia asked, "Why don't we just get Uncle Raymond involved and let him take care of all of this?"

"Because Uncle Raymond is a by-the-book guy. I'm sure Dad told him about his suspicions, or if he didn't, he had his reasons. My job . . . Our job is to find out what Dad knew, and then we can decide whether or not we need to inform Uncle Raymond."

"For all we know, he might already know something," Montana added.

"You promised," Savannah said.

Montana placed the folder down on the table. "I haven't told Uncle Raymond anything. But come on. He's a smart man. He should know we—well, you—aren't sitting idly by while a killer is loose."

"Has it ever crossed your mind as to why Uncle Raymond has never talked to us about finding the killer?" Savannah asked.

"Because maybe he knows and is just waiting to get enough evidence," Asia added.

"Could be. But for now, let's just keep this between us."

The doorbell rang. "Were either one of you expecting anyone?" Savannah asked.

"No," Montana and Asia said in unison.

"Grab your weapons," Savannah said as she stood to go answer the door.

Savannah saw Asia reach for her small handgun.

She heard Montana say, "She better be kidding."

"Better safe than sorry," Asia responded.

Savannah looked through the peephole. To her relief it was Troy; however, she was upset at him because she specifically told him she would call when her sisters left. She glanced at the clock on the foyer wall. The time was ten o'clock. She didn't realize they had been talking this long. The doorbell rang again.

Montana walked behind her. "Do we need to pull out the heavy artillery, or are you going to open the door?"

Savannah shooed her away with her hand. "I got it."

She opened the door. Without an invitation Troy entered, dressed in a pair of black jeans and black button-down shirt. "What a welcome party," Troy joked.

Savannah's heart skipped a beat. Her hand remained on the door as she turned around and saw both of her sisters with their weapons by their side. Her voice crackled. "We weren't expecting company."

"Obviously."

Asia cleared her throat. "Excuse my rude sister. I'm Asia."

"You're the youngest, right?"

While they were introducing themselves, Savannah rushed to remove their notes and to get her nerves together. By the time they made it back to the living room, the table was nice and neat.

"You didn't have to clean up on my account," Bridges commented. The sparkle in his eyes lit up when he looked at Savannah.

Asia and Montana looked from one to the other.

"Did we miss something?" Montana asked.

"No, but my, my, my, it's getting late and you both have to get up early," Savannah said, walking toward the center of the doorway.

"I can spend the night over here in my old room," Asia suggested.

"Or not," Montana said. "Can't you see she wants some time alone with her new beau?"

"He's not my beau. Besides, he has somebody."

"No, I don't," Bridges shouted from behind.

Savannah grabbed Asia by the arm and literally had to pull her from in front of Troy. "I'll be back," Savannah mouthed.

Troy laughed.

"He's off-limits, Asia." Savannah felt possessive, although they were no longer a couple. Now, if she could get her heart to remember that fact, she would be better off.

"You didn't tell us he was cute," Asia said.

Montana added, "And fine."

"You didn't ask. Now bye. Talk to you two tomorrow."

Montana and Asia got a good laugh at her expense. Montana pretended to be offended. "We've been kicked to the curb because of a man. I never would have believed it."

"Out now!" Savannah shouted. She loved her sisters, but at times they could be pests. She watched them enter their cars. She didn't see Troy's vehicle. She dreaded the questions her sisters would have after tonight about Troy.

~ 6 ~

Savannah walked back in the living room after they left. "See what you started."

Troy couldn't hold back his laughter. "I didn't mean to embarrass you, but you should have called me."

Savannah picked up a pillow and threw it at him. He ducked a little too late. "What was so important that it couldn't wait until tomorrow?"

Troy sat down on the couch next to her. "I reviewed the information you gave me last night, and I also had a chance to make a few phone calls."

Troy went over what he had discovered through his phone calls. "We need to get those papers from your dad's safe-deposit box, and that'll probably solve the whole puzzle."

Before Savannah could respond, the lights went out. "I hope I have an extra fuse."

Savannah left Troy in the living room as she felt her way to the kitchen. She searched through the kitchen drawers to locate her flashlight and fuse. "Come on. It has to be in here somewhere," she said out loud.

She smelled Troy's cologne before he opened his mouth. "I don't think it's a fuse. I heard something outside and wanted to make sure you were okay."

"I'm fine," she responded.

A noise came from the direction of the living room. Troy automatically went for his weapon. He held up his index finger to his mouth and mouthed the word, "Quiet."

Savannah recalled the men in black's surprise visit earlier during the day. She leaned and whispered in Troy's ear, "Some men stopped by the house earlier today. I don't know who they were, but they gave me the jitters."

"I wish you would have mentioned it earlier."

Savannah opened her mouth to speak but was thrown to the floor by Troy. Before she could blink, a smoke bomb flew through the kitchen window shattering glass everywhere.

Troy grabbed her by the arm. "Follow me."

Smoke filled the room, making their vision cloudy.

Savannah snapped. "Why do I have to follow you? This is my house. You need to follow me."

"I'm not going to argue with you. Get us to the nearest exit," Troy said as he reluctantly let Savannah lead them out of the kitchen.

She opened the side door. Troy said, "No, it's not safe. Find us another way."

Savannah grabbed Troy's hand and pulled him in another direction. She knew exactly where they were going. She led them to the secret panic room her dad had built in the house many years ago. Her father made sure they had safety drills, and fortunately, up until this moment, she had never had to retreat there. Not knowing what or who was on the outside trying to get in, she rushed with Troy behind her to the secret hideaway.

"Well, I'll be," Troy said as he helped Savannah move things out of a closet and rearrange them so they wouldn't look disturbed.

Savannah shone the flashlight on a panel near the secret door and activated a code. She led them down the stairs.

Troy watched Savannah as she hit a switch and the entire room lit up. Instead of being a stuffy room, it was filled with state-of-the-art equipment and appeared more like a den rather than an underground dungeon.

She flipped on a security monitor. He looked at it to see if he could recognize the assailants. While he watched the monitor, Savannah removed some weapons from a glass rack on the wall. "Just in case you need this." She handed him an assault rifle.

"And here I thought I had to protect you."

"Now is not the time for jokes." Savannah's tone was more of being scared than being angry.

"Just trying to lighten things up," Troy responded. "We need to get out of here. There are four that I can see, and they are going from room to room."

"They'll never find us."

"I'm sure they won't, but we don't want to be trapped here, just in case."

"There's a secret passageway that'll bring us to the other street," Savannah said as she picked up a backpack and placed a few more items in it, including additional ammunition and the flashlight she got from the kitchen.

"Good. That'll put us closer to my car," he said.

"I meant to ask where you were parked."

"Fortunately for us, I thought it best to check out the surroundings before dropping by."

Savannah glanced at the security cameras. "I've activated the alarm, so the cops should be here any minute. Follow me."

"After you." Troy extended his hand and followed Savannah through the tunnel.

Savannah stopped several times. She held her hand up to her nose. "I think I'm going to puke." The stench smelled like a combination of moldy mildew and dead animals.

Troy gave her a handkerchief out of his pocket. "Hold this up to your nose."

They continued down the pathway until they reached a ladder. "This is it," Savannah said. She removed the backpack and handed it to him. She climbed up first. The round metal didn't bulge.

"Let me," Troy said. Savannah was in the process of going back down the ladder, and her buttocks ended up in Troy's face.

"Now that's a new meaning to kiss my—"

Savannah interrupted him, "Sorry."

Troy backed down and helped Savannah when she reached the last step. She jumped off and landed face-to-face with Troy. Time stood still as they stared into each other's eyes. Troy's vibrating phone broke the trance.

"We better get going," he said, ignoring the phone call. Savannah moved out of the way as she watched Troy climb up the ladder. With a few hard pushes he was able to open the metal. He looked around, and when he was sure all was secure, he motioned with his hand for her to follow suit.

She picked up the backpack and handed it to him right before he helped her out of the hole. He quickly placed the metal back over the hole and covered it back up with the grass. "Come on. I'm parked not far from here."

The adrenaline rush Savannah felt had her on edge. She was glad she worked out regularly or she wouldn't have been able to keep up with Troy's fast pace.

He opened the door to his SUV for Savannah before rushing to the driver's side. Savannah was impressed that even in times of distress he was still a gentleman.

If it weren't for their history, she would find his noble ways sexy. She got in and put on her seat belt.

"Whoever is after you will soon realize you're not in the house."

Although it felt like hours since escaping into the secret room, only minutes had passed.

"I need to use your phone."

"Under the circumstances I think you need to keep communication with anyone at a minimum," Troy responded.

"Either let me use your phone, or let me off at the first pay phone," Savannah snapped. "I need to make sure my sisters are okay."

Troy had been so concerned with Savannah's safety, he had forgotten about her sisters. He couldn't let anything happen to her or them. Major would never forgive him if he did. Funny, how a dead man could still control him from the grave. Not wanting to be caught off guard again, Troy decided at the last minute to go down Savannah's street. He hit a button and Savannah's seat went straight back.

"What in the world!" Savannah shouted.

"I want to see if your houseguests are still there, and see if I can get a license plate number."

Savannah let out a few obscenities as she dialed Montana's number. She was barely talking above a whisper. Troy slowed down his car enough to see that the assailants were still snooping around. He made a mental note of the license plate and was tempted to stop, until he saw several shadowy figures exit the backyard. Troy continued to drive at a normal pace, so as not to draw attention. At the sound of the police sirens, it looked as if both he and the assailants had escaped just in time.

"I'm okay. Stop worrying," Savannah repeated several times.

Troy tried not to listen to her private conversation. A part of him envied the closeness she seemed to have with her sisters. His thoughts lingered on distant memories of his mom and sister.

Troy heard Savannah say, "Call me on the number displayed on your caller ID if you need anything." She hung up the phone and sighed. "All is secure. I told them I would be staying with you tonight."

Lucky me, Troy thought.

~ 7 ~

Savannah marveled at the beautiful landscaping outside Troy's two-story brick home. She remained silent as he pulled into a three-car garage. The lights turned on, revealing a black sports car and a white sedan. Troy reached the passenger door before she could exit. The loud sound of the closing garage door almost drowned out her voice as she said, "Thanks."

"Glad to be of service."

Troy led her inside, into a spacious kitchen. "You live alone?" she asked.

"Most of the time," Troy responded.

"What is that supposed to mean?" Savannah didn't mean to ask her question out loud.

"The lady cares," Troy said as he deactivated his alarm. "Are you hungry?"

"No, I just want to lie down," Savannah responded.

"You can have my room," he volunteered.

"I'm sure with a big old house like this, you have a guest room."

"I do, but you're more than just a guest." The way his words seemed to fall sensuously out of his mouth caught Savannah by surprise.

Savannah half listened to Troy as they walked through the house. She admired the artwork on the walls. A beautiful gold-trimmed chandelier hung above the winding staircase. The temptation to remove her shoes and walk barefoot on the thick plush carpet almost overtook her.

Troy opened the door to a room twice as big as her bedroom. Savannah assumed Troy's favorite color was black, because the entire room's decor was ebony furniture and accessories. On the thick comforter an illustration of a black panther with piercing eyes stared back at her. She was so tired, that all she wanted to do was plop down on the bed.

Savannah gasped as she saw her sweaty reflection staring back at her from the dresser mirror. "I hate to bother you, but if you have a T-shirt or something I can borrow until tomorrow. I want to take a bath before calling it a night."

"I'm one step ahead of you," Troy responded. He removed a black-and-gold T-shirt with the New Orleans Saints Super Bowl emblem across the front.

She frowned because she was a Dallas Cowboys fan. "It figures. I need some towels too."

"Did anyone ever tell you, you were bossy?"

"My sisters tell me that all of the time," Savannah said as she followed him to the master bathroom.

Savannah's eyes bucked when she saw two sinks trimmed in sterling silver and "his and her" toilets. What impressed Savannah the most was the deep tub, which seemed to be calling her name.

"Here are your towels and some soap. If you need anything else, just yell," Troy stated before exiting the bathroom.

Savannah smiled for the first time since being ousted out of her house. "I think I got it from here."

She waited for him to exit and locked the door as soon as the door was closed.

"I'm not going to bother you," Troy said loudly.

The steam from the hot bathwater fogged up the windows. Savannah thought about the events that transpired in the past twenty-four hours. Her muscles relaxed, releasing the tension throughout her body as she eased herself into the hot, bubbly water.

She leaned back and closed her eyes. Was she in over her head? Should she give up her quest to find her dad's killer? Who were the people who broke into her house? What were they looking for? It dawned on her that she left the folder with the information in a secret compartment within the fireplace. She hoped they didn't look there. She hid it when she was trying to get rid of the information when Troy first arrived.

The knock on the door broke Savannah out of her deep thoughts.

"Just checking to make sure you're okay in there," Troy spoke firmly so she could hear.

"I'm fine. I'll be out soon."

The water's cool temperature alerted Savannah that she had been in the bath a long time and jolted her awake. She took her time getting out of the tub. Her body signaled she was more tired than she imagined. Not trying to be nosy, she searched through the cabinets in search of a tube of deodorant. A cabinet could tell a lot about a person. She noticed many hygiene products and cleaning products. She picked up an unopened box of condoms before throwing it back onto the shelf. Her search was not in vain. She located a new tube of deodorant and rubbed some under her arms.

Savannah pulled the long black T-shirt Troy had given her over her head. She cringed at the sight of her unruly curly hair tossed across her head. Standing before the mirror, she braided her hair into one long braid before exiting the bathroom. Troy was nowhere around. The bed was turned down and there was a glass and a bottle of water on a tray by the bed. She opened the seal of the bottle and took a sip. The soft bed welcomed her, and she fell asleep as soon as her head hit the pillows.

Savannah didn't know how long she had been asleep. When she woke up, she felt out of place. *Where am I? Why am I in a strange bed?* It took her a few seconds to gather her senses. The memory from last night rushed back to her. She jumped out of bed, looking for her clothes. Although they were not clean, it was all she had to put on. To her surprise they were washed and dried and folded up, placed on a chair on the opposite end of the bed.

"When did he find the time?" she asked out loud.

She pulled the clothes up to her nose and inhaled the freshly washed scent. A knock on the door interrupted her thoughts. "Are you up?" Troy asked.

"I'll be dressed in a minute," she responded.

She placed the Saints T-shirt on the chair. When she opened the door, Troy was nowhere to be found. She called out his name a few times but didn't get a response. She wandered down the hall and leaned on the rail. She stopped to admire the downstairs view from the banister.

Troy walked in view and looked up. "I cooked a big breakfast, just in case you're hungry."

Savannah was starving. Her growling stomach would have betrayed her if she tried to deny it. Troy waited for her at the end of the stairway.

"Thanks for washing my clothes," Savannah said.

"You're quite welcome. Your food awaits," he said as he extended his arm.

Savannah wrapped her arm through his and allowed him to guide her into the kitchen. "This smells good. I don't know where to begin."

Savannah and Troy ate without talking about last night's events. Savannah stood to clear the table. Troy said, "Don't worry about the dishes. I got it."

"But—"

"No buts. You're a guest."

"But last night you said—"

"Speaking of last night," Troy said as he took the dishes from the table to the sink. "I think you better call your sisters. Montana left a message on my phone about the cops calling her. She sounded a little frantic, so it was hard to make out exactly what she said."

Savannah frowned. "Why didn't you tell me?"

"You needed to eat."

Savannah saw the phone near the door. "After I find out what's going on, I need you to take me home immediately."

Troy saluted her. "Yes, ma'am."

Troy had no right to make decisions for her. He should have told her about Montana's call. Savannah tried to calm down while waiting for Montana to answer her cell phone. She was unsuccessful reaching her. The call went to voice mail. She dialed Asia's number. She watched Troy clean up the kitchen as she nervously tapped her foot. "Asia, what's going on?"

Before Asia could respond, Montana's voice rang out from the other end. "The police said the house looked a mess. We've been trying to reach you. Neither one of us has slept a wink worried about you."

"I told you I was fine. Look, don't go over to the house. Give me the number of the officer you spoke with and I'll take it from here."

"I want you to know I called Uncle Raymond."

"Montana, I told you I got this."

"He's out of the country right now. But as soon as he calls me back, I'm telling him everything."

"Don't. I need you to trust me. Do not say anything to him or anybody else. Please," Savannah pleaded.

"This is too much," Montana responded.

"Let me talk to Asia," Savannah stated.

"Sis, what's going on?" Asia asked. "We've been worried sick about you."

"I need you to convince Montana not to talk to Uncle Raymond. I'm not saying he had anything to do with Dad's death, but he works for The Agency. He might be the enemy."

"I can't promise you she'll listen to me, but I'll do my best," Asia promised.

~ 8 ~

Troy watched Savannah frantically pace side to side as she talked to her sisters. He knew he should have told her before breakfast about the message, but neither he nor she had had much sleep, and he wanted her to be relaxed for at least a few minutes. Selfishly he wanted to enjoy some uninterrupted time with her.

I need to get a grip. That's why I don't like mixing business with pleasure. Truth be told, he knew from the moment he laid eyes on Savannah again, he needed her. Troy wanted her like he needed oxygen.

He told Savannah almost everything.

He purposely left out the fact that Major made him promise to watch out for Savannah and her sisters if anything happened to him. He recalled their last conversation as if Major had a premonition of his death.

They met at a local diner and talked over coffee. Troy could hear Major's voice as if he said it yesterday. "There's a rat in The Agency who has been getting some of the other operatives killed."

"Are you sure? I know we have a few hotheads— myself included—but a rat? Major, that's serious."

Major pulled out a small brown envelope. He checked his surroundings before sliding it to Troy under the table. Troy took it and slipped it into his pant pocket without anyone being the wiser.

"Take a look at it, and then let me know what you think."

"I will, but I don't think you have anything to worry about," Troy said in between bites.

"I'm counting on you to take care of my daughters, especially Savannah."

"Do your girls know about me?" Troy asked.

"No, I've tried to keep as much of my job from them as possible."

"Maybe you should tell at least one of them, so it won't be a surprise."

"Son, you handle your business and I'll handle mine. Understood?" Major asked.

"Yes, sir."

Troy never brought it up again. He assumed that Major would be around and die a natural death. He didn't expect foul play to be the end of his friend and ex-boss.

"Troy, one more thing. When are you going to make things right with my daughter?" Major asked.

Troy was caught totally off guard. Up until this point he assumed Major didn't know about his connection to Savannah. He stuttered, *"I'm n-not the right man for her."*

"Let me be the judge of that. From what I see, you're the only man whom I feel worthy of being with my daughter."

"But, sir, you don't understand. There's no way Savannah would take me back."

Major looked him in the eyes. *"When the time is right, Savannah will welcome you back into her life."*

Troy hadn't believed Major then, but now he did have some hope. Savannah wasn't throwing things at him or cursing him out, so maybe, just maybe, he had a chance of winning Savannah's heart again.

"Earth to Troy." Savannah tapped him on his shoulder.

"Sorry, my mind was a million miles away."

"Whatever. I need you to take me home."

"Before you go home, we need to talk."

"We can talk in the car," Savannah responded.

"Give me a few minutes and we can leave."

"While you're doing that, I have one more phone call to make." Savannah dismissed him as if he weren't there.

While Savannah made her phone call, Troy went to his safe and removed some items that he hoped he wouldn't need. Just in case they ran into some trouble, he wanted to be safe and not regret anything later.

Troy returned to the room. "Let's go," he said.

Savannah followed him into the garage. He opened her door and before long they were headed to Savannah's.

Savannah didn't hesitate to reach over and turn his radio to another station.

"I wish you wouldn't do that," he said.

"Bad habit" was all Savannah would say.

"Let's make a deal. When we're in your car, we'll listen to your music. While we're in mine, we'll listen to what I want."

Savannah rolled her eyes. He could see her lips turn into a slight smile. It was just like old times. Maybe the ice was breaking. Savannah didn't say anything; instead, she turned and looked out the window. Troy felt like he achieved a small victory. They missed rush-hour traffic by an hour, so Troy made it to her house in record time.

Before he could bring the car to a complete stop in her driveway, Savannah had opened her door. She rushed to the African American policeman's side. Troy parked the car and jumped out to catch up with her.

"I'm Officer Nash and that's my partner, Officer Pendleton."

Officer Pendleton, a man who was one doughnut short of being overweight, addressed Troy. "Can we see some identification—"

"I don't think all of that's necessary," Savannah interrupted. "He's a friend of mine."

Officer Pendleton looked at Nash for approval. "Fine. Let's go inside for a moment."

Savannah didn't need a key to get in because the front door was unlocked. She gasped when she saw everything thrown in the various rooms.

Troy did his best to support her by not letting her from his side.

"Your neighbor gave us descriptions of two guys who stopped by here yesterday morning," Officer Nash stated.

"I didn't get a good look at them. All I can tell you is they were in a black sedan."

Officer Pendleton asked, "Why didn't you call us?"

"I don't mean to be disrespectful, Officer, but the emergency alert you received was my way of communicating. I set it off before getting my butt quickly out of the house."

"I got this," Officer Nash said to his partner. He turned to face Savannah. "Do you think you can tell us everything you remember from last night?"

Savannah recited last night's event, excluding the information about their exact escape.

After the officers left, Savannah stood in the doorway and didn't move. Troy felt compelled to reach out to her. He wrapped his arms around her and held her until she got the strength to start the cleanup process.

He kissed the top of her head. "You're not in this alone."

"I don't even know where to begin."

"You take upstairs and I'll take the downstairs and we'll meet up somewhere in the middle," Troy said, attempting to lighten up the situation.

"You're sure you're not an angel. One minute I want to hit you, and the next minute I want to give you a hug."

"I'll take the hug," Troy responded.

Savannah wiped her teary eyes. "Just put stuff back, the best you can. I'll do a thorough cleanup later."

Before they could act on their cleanup duty, the doorknob turned. Troy pushed Savannah behind him as he removed his gun. Asia and Montana walked in at the same moment Troy had unlocked the safety and was ready to shoot.

"Man, you guys could have been killed!" Savannah shouted. She walked past Troy and hugged her sisters.

"We weren't going to let you deal with this by yourself. This is our problem too," Montana said, not once loosening her hug.

Troy watched the encounter. "Ladies, I don't mean to impose, but you might want to close the door."

Asia was the first to leave the group hug. "This place is a mess," she said as she walked past them all.

"We were just about to straighten up." Savannah closed and locked the door.

"Help is here." Montana picked up pillows off the floor as she talked. "Troy, it's good seeing you again."

"Same here. Just wish it were under other circumstances."

"I know what you mean," Asia responded.

Savannah and Troy took the downstairs, while Montana and Asia cleaned upstairs. Troy did a thorough sweep for bugging devices and was relieved to find none.

"I'm sure they'll be back. The information they were looking for was here." Savannah made a beeline to the fireplace. She reached her hand up the chimney and removed some folders.

"When did you have time to do that?" Troy asked out of curiosity.

"A lady can never reveal all of her secrets." Her eyes twinkled as she smiled.

"I'm just glad they didn't break anything," Montana stated as she walked into the room.

"It could have been worse." *One of us could have been killed,* Savannah thought.

"I don't know about y'all, but I've worked up an appetite." Troy rubbed his stomach. "What do you ladies like? I'll go pick us up something."

After taking their orders, Troy heard Montana say, "I like him. He's a keeper."

He didn't wait to hear what Savannah's response would be.

~ *9* ~

While waiting for Troy to return, the three sisters sat in the living room. The tension was thicker than molasses. Savannah felt responsible for the fear she knew her sisters now faced. "Ladies, this is getting dangerous. I think we should all move under one roof," Savannah suggested.

"Not here," Montana responded. She looked around the room. "Do you actually think we would be safe here?"

Savannah hung her head. She didn't know what to think. "Until I can get a better handle on things, I think it's best. First order of business, you both need to take a leave of absence."

Asia, who normally agreed with Savannah, threw her hands up in disgust. "You must have hit your head while you were trying to escape last night."

"Vanna, what we need to do is leave this to Uncle Raymond," Montana said.

Savannah felt trapped. "Doesn't it seem strange that Dad didn't confide his suspicions with Uncle Raymond? Apparently, he didn't trust him, so neither should we."

Asia stood up. "I'm out of here. Montana's right. You are beyond obsessed." Asia looked between Savannah and Montana. "You both are welcome to stay with me." Asia looked for her purse and keys. "I'm out of here."

Montana cleared her throat before holding up a key ring with several keys. "You rode with me."

Asia plopped back on the couch without saying a word.

"Now that your temper tantrum is out of the way, maybe you'll listen," Savannah stated.

Asia crossed her arms, leaned back in her chair, and rolled her eyes.

Montana would have been amused under normal circumstances, but so much was at stake, including their lives. "Vanna, I'm at a loss. At this point I don't know what to do. I fear for our safety."

Savannah stood up as if she was preparing to give a lecture. She glanced at the clock. "Troy will be back soon, so let me get right to it. First, make sure you are strapped with your gun at all times. Whether you're sleeping, eating, or even using the restroom."

Asia looked at the floor instead of directly at Savannah. Savannah pulled out her notebook. "I changed the code to the secret room. It's two, four, nine and one.. Memorize it. Asia, I need for you to hack into The Agency's system." She pulled out a sheet of paper with some names on it and handed it to her. "I need for you to find out as much as you can on the people on the list."

Asia stared at it and a curve formed at the corners of her mouth. "It's as good as done."

Savannah continued to give out orders. "Montana, I need for you to get us some gear. Dad has some here, but this might not be enough."

"I don't know, Vanna. I have a funny feeling about all of this."

"Do you want to play the victim, or be the victor?" Savanna asked.

"A victim, I'm not," Montana responded.

"Then it's settled. We might need to change our appearances, so I'll leave that up to you too."

The knock at the door was very faint. If Savannah hadn't been looking for Troy to return, she wouldn't have heard it. She drew her weapon. Her sisters followed suit. She walked to the door and heard Troy's voice. She motioned for her sisters to put their weapons away.

She opened the door and assisted Troy in bringing in the bags of food. She whispered, "Thanks for giving me a little extra time with my sisters."

He winked his right eye.

Small talk was made as they devoured the Chinese food. Asia opened up her fortune cookie and read it out loud. "'Beware of strangers.'"

They all laughed. Savannah opened up hers next. "'Keep an open eye and an open heart.'" She balled up the paper and threw it down. "I never get any good ones."

Montana read hers. "'Trust one, not all.'"

"Troy, your turn," Asia said.

"Oh no. I don't believe in those things."

"We just do it for the fun of it," Savannah said.

"Come on. You're scared," Asia challenged him.

"The things a man does for a woman." His eyes were on Savannah. Montana and Asia looked at the exchange. Troy opened up his fortune cookie. "'What you're looking for is staring you in the face.'" He threw it on the table. "See, a bunch of junk."

Asia retrieved the paper and read it out loud again. She looked between Savannah and Troy. "You two have to be in some serious denial. Even the fortune cookies can see it."

Savannah faked innocence. She put her right hand across her chest. "What? What did I do?"

"Nothing. I'll drop it for now." Asia got up and, with the help of Montana, cleared the table.

"You have to forgive Asia. She can be a little annoying at times," Savannah said.

Asia yelled from behind her, "I heard that!"

They laughed. Troy rubbed his stomach. "It's been a while since I had some good shrimp fried rice."

"Our dad used to take us there at least once a month." Savannah's eyes glazed over. For a moment she was transported back in time. She recalled one of the last times they shared a meal at Cheung's.

Troy handed her a napkin. "Thanks," she responded as she wiped her watery eyes.

Troy glanced at his watch. "We still have time to make it to the bank."

"For a moment I thought you were human. You only care about one thing." Savannah pushed her chair out and stormed away from the table.

Troy rushed behind her. He tried to grab her, but she wouldn't relent. "Don't touch me."

Troy held his hands up in defense. "Vanna, I don't know what's gotten into you—"

"You're what's gotten to me," she interrupted. She ran up the stairs, not caring how her dramatic exit confused not only Troy, but also her sisters, who were standing behind him.

The reflection in the mirror staring back at her frightened her. She was normally poised and had to be the strong one for her sisters. It seemed that she was falling apart at the seams. She turned on the cold water and splashed some on her face. She wiped her face with a towel.

"Vanna, may I come in?" Montana asked from the other side of the door.

"Go away," she responded. Savannah was still not ready to share with Montana the true dynamics of her and Troy's relationship.

"Open the door," Montana demanded.

"I'm okay. Just give me a minute." Savannah redid the braid in her hair before exiting the bathroom. Montana wasn't waiting on the other side. She sighed. She walked at a snail's pace back down the stairs.

A hush fell over the living room when she walked in. Troy was sitting on the love seat, while her sisters were each sitting on opposite ends of the couch. Savannah took a seat in the lone chair.

"Your sisters were telling me about some of your plans," Troy said.

Savannah felt betrayed. Troy was an outsider, and her sisters shouldn't have been discussing their plans with him, or anyone else. She tried not to show her annoyance.

Montana spoke next. "Troy has convinced us that we should all stay here."

Asia added, "This will be like our command central."

"Thanks, Troy." Savannah crossed her arms and leaned back in her chair.

She listened to them go on and on about their plans, as if it weren't her idea to start with.

"Enough already!" she yelled.

The room once again got silent.

Troy intervened. "I'm sorry if you feel like I stepped on your toes."

"By all means, I'm glad, with my short stint in the bathroom, you had time to bond."

The house phone rang. Montana looked at the caller ID. "It's Uncle Raymond."

"Don't answer it," Troy said.

Savannah stood up and took the phone from Montana. "I'm still the queen of this abode," she snarled. "Hello."

She turned her back to Troy and her sisters. "No, everything is fine," she lied. She turned around to look at Montana. "She was just having one of her moments. She's here now. She said she'll call you back later." A few seconds later, Savannah disconnected the call.

10

"Savannah, you might be mad at me, but please don't take it out on your sisters," Troy stood and said.

"You're so conceited." She threw her hands up in the air. "I answered the call because if I wouldn't have, he would have been trying to track us down, and at this point I'm trying not to get him involved."

Asia said, "Don't you think you should tell her."

"You talk too much," Montana snapped.

Savannah walked and stood near the sofa. "What is she talking about?" Savannah tapped her foot. "We don't have all day. I have to leave for the bank in a minute, if I'm going to get there before they close."

"Nothing," Montana responded.

Savannah grabbed her purse and stormed toward the kitchen.

"Ladies, I'll be back. Lock up. Activate the alarm," Troy said as he rushed behind Savannah.

Savannah was opening the garage door when Troy entered. "Savannah, stop," he asserted.

"You don't need to come with me. Stay and protect my sisters. I don't need your protection," Savannah snapped.

"You might not, but you do need me to be an extra set of eyes."

It appeared as if Savannah thought about it for a moment. She unlocked the passenger door. "Get in!" she yelled.

The tension between the two didn't dissolve during the less than fifteen minutes it took to get to the bank. "Your sisters are only trying to make things easier for you, you know," Troy said.

"I didn't ask you," Savannah snapped.

"I just don't like feeling this tension between you all. Between us." Troy said the last barely above a whisper. He knew she heard him because the light in her eyes sparkled for a few seconds.

Before either could say anything else on the subject, Savannah was pulling up in the bank's parking lot. She removed her gun and placed it in the divider between the seats. "Just in case there's a metal detector."

"I got your back."

"If I'm in there longer than thirty minutes, come in shooting," Savannah joked.

Troy felt relieved that she was at least joking with him now. He handed her a pen. "If for some reason you run into any trouble, push the top of the pen and it'll signal me."

"Thanks," she said as she exited the car.

Savannah's stomach turned flips as she entered the bank. She tried to act normal. She tried to act like the information she was coming to retrieve meant nothing. The information in the safe-deposit box could possibly be all she needed to determine who had killed her father.

After she showed proper ID, the bank branch manager led her into the room where the safe-deposit boxes were kept. He entered a code and she used the key she had to open the box.

"I'll be outside if you need me," he said, leaving her there to go through it without being watched.

She sat at the table and removed some of the items. She held both her parents' wedding rings. "Mama, why did you have to die so young?" Savannah wept.

She wiped the tears from her eyes. She felt like she was prying into her parents' private life. She looked at the pictures and other items. So far, she didn't see anything in it related to her father's old job.

"Voila," she said when she found a brown envelope. She read the enclosed letter first, and could hear her father's voice in her mind as she read.

My dearest Savannah,

If you're reading this, it means that someone got to me before I could get to the bottom of things. As much as I want you to seek justice on the person or people behind me not being there with my girls, I do not, under any circumstances, want you risking your life. The information on this disc should be handed to one person, and that's Troy Bridges. By now, you've probably met. I just hope you haven't hurt him (smile). Troy can help you get justice. If by chance someone is coming after you because they suspect you know more than you do, then promise me that you and your sisters will use the skills I taught you. My enemies will underestimate you because you are women, but I have full confidence that you will prove them wrong. Before giving the disc to Troy, make sure Asia makes a copy. Tell her to use the secure path. She'll know what I'm talking about. It pains me to write this letter, but I didn't want to leave you without the tools to solve my murder. I love you. Take care of yourself and your sisters. I've also enclosed separate letters for Montana and for Asia. Please give those to them. Love you all.

Love,
Dad

P.S. Take care of Troy too. He doesn't realize it, but he needs you just as much as you need him. Please find it in your heart to forgive him. He was young and scared. Under the circumstances he did the right thing.

Savannah placed the disc and the brown envelope with the letter in her purse. She placed the remaining items back in the safe-deposit box. She signaled for the bank manager and watched him secure the box back in its place.

With the disc and letters from her dad, Savannah felt better about the path she had taken. She would hold on to the disc until Asia was able to make a copy, and then she would turn it over to Troy. She wondered how her father knew about Troy. She wasn't sure she could give him another chance. What she wanted to do to Troy would land her in jail.

"I was about to send in the cavalry to get you," Troy teased as Savannah was safely buckled behind the steering wheel.

"No, all's well." Savannah refused to look him in the eyes. "I'm sure my sisters are worried."

"They love you."

"I know," Savannah responded as she pulled out of the parking lot.

Savannah decided to turn on some music, with hopes of avoiding a conversation with Troy. "Good system," Troy said, once they pulled up into the garage.

Savannah pretended not to hear. She didn't wait for him to exit the car. She jumped out, and he was on her heels as she walked into the kitchen. Montana and Asia were nowhere to be found.

"Wait here," Savannah directed.

"I need to make a few phone calls, anyway," Troy responded.

"She asked you to wait, but you wouldn't listen. What if she's right? What if he knows something that led to Dad's death," Savannah overheard Asia say when she made it to the top of the stairway.

"Savannah, can be hot-headed. When she told us her plans, I didn't think there was anything wrong with talking to Uncle Raymond. I never thought this would happen ."

Savannah was livid. "You idiot! I told you not to talk to Uncle Raymond. Now it explains why those men broke in here."

Montana's body shivered. "I'm sorry. I didn't know."

Savannah removed the brown envelope from her purse. She threw the letter at Montana. "Sorry is not good enough."

Montana bent down and retrieved the letter from the floor. Tears flowed down her cheeks as she read it. Asia took the letter from Montana.

Savannah watched them read it. "Satisfied?"

Between sniffles Montana said, "It still doesn't prove anything."

"Maybe not. Asia, here's the disc. Please copy it so I can give it to Troy."

"I'll be in our secret place," Asia responded.

Montana was behind Asia. "Don't move!" Savannah yelled.

"I was going to help out," she responded as her voice crackled.

Savannah closed the door behind Asia. "Here's your letter from Dad." She handed her a sealed letter. Savannah knew Montana thought she was going to go off on her for talking to Uncle Raymond. Although she should, Savannah knew that reading the note in her father's handwriting probably was more than enough guilt.

Montana read the note out loud.

"'My sweet Montana, Words could not express how much I love you and your sisters. I hope you're not taking out your frustrations on your sisters. This is the time you all need to pull together. You're more like your mother, Ellen, than you'll ever know. She could be pigheaded, but I loved that woman. Before I digress, I don't want you to close out your heart. I know it's hard for you to trust people. Trust your sisters and trust the love that your mother and I had for you. No matter what happens, know that you were loved.'"

Montana dropped the letter on the bed. "I can't read any more." She wept, and Savannah rocked her back and forth in her arms. They stayed in that position until someone knocked on the door.

11

Troy turned to walk away right before Savannah opened the bedroom door. "I need to head out, but wanted to make sure all was secure here. I'll be checking on you all later."

Savannah said, "Let me walk you out."

Troy followed Savannah down the stairs. "I ran into Asia downstairs and she told me it was okay."

"It's fine," Savannah said as she waved her hand.

Troy walked to the front door. "If you need anything, and I do mean *anything,* don't hesitate to call me. Make sure you sleep in shifts. Activate the alarm as soon as I leave."

Savannah saluted him. "Yes, sir."

Troy paused. Savannah placed one hand on the doorknob. "You're not going to ask?"

"When you're ready to share the contents of the safe-deposit box, you'll share."

Savannah leaned on the door. "What are you not telling me?"

"Tomorrow at zero nine hundred I'll meet you here."

Troy reached around Savannah for the doorknob. He could feel the heat coming from her body, or was it his?

"Tomorrow," she said as she moved and allowed him out the door.

Troy couldn't hold back a smile. Although he and Savannah seemed to be like oil and water, there was something about her that made him want to protect then set up a meeting.

"Okay, boss."

"Man, you know I hate it when you call me that."

"Get used to it. Business is booming."

"Sad for them, but good for us."

Parker sat across the desk from Troy. He updated Troy on a few more cases. "Do you need any additional manpower on that special case you're working on?"

Troy wasn't sure if he should disclose what he was working on with everyone yet. The less information folks knew, the better. Some still had ties with The Agency, and he didn't want it leaked that he was investigating there. "No, I got it. It's just a favor for a friend. I'll be out for the next few days, though. If you can hold it down here for me, I'd appreciate it."

"I got your back. Just call me if you need me."

"Will do." They shook hands. Parker left Troy alone with his thoughts.

Troy checked his voice mail. He made notes as he listened. The final voice mail made the hair on the back of his neck stand up. "Relentless, I heard you've been in contact with Savannah."

Troy said all sorts of curse words. This was the last thing they needed. Hopefully, he could talk to Commander Raymond Steel without him blowing his connection with Savannah and her sisters out of proportion. He never felt the need to check in with anybody before, but before he called his ex-commander back, he needed to talk to Savannah. He phoned her to discuss this development.

"Your uncle knows I've been in contact with you."

"I know."

Troy balled up the paper in his hands. "When were you going to tell me? I thought we were going to keep our liaison a secret."

It sounded like the phone was muffled. "Montana took it upon herself to tell him more than she should have."

Troy didn't like the direction the conversation was heading. "What exactly did she say? Word for word."

"I'll let her tell you."

Montana came on the phone a few seconds later. "I'm sorry, Troy. I was scared and he's been our uncle since forever."

"Calm down," he said in a soothing voice, although he was infuriated with her.

"I only told him that you helped Savannah get away when those guys broke in the other night."

"Anything else you're not saying?"

"He did say you were bad news and that we should stay as far away from you as possible."

"Figures. Let me talk to Savannah," he said, dismissing Montana, but not trying to sound annoyed.

Savannah said, "You got more out of her than I did."

"Look, Savannah. When he asks, because he will ask, tell him I stopped by because I was feeling nostalgic about Major. I just happened to be there when the burglars came."

"Sounds like a feasible story to me."

"I got to make a call."

He dreaded dialing the numbers, but it was best that he got it over with. "May I speak with Commander Steel, please? This is Relentless."

"What's the word?"

Troy wasn't up on the new password. He had to think on his feet. "I'm a former op. I'm returning his call."

"Hold, please."

Steel immediately went into a rant. "If one hair gets hurt on my girls' heads, your head is mine."

"Hello to you too." Troy twirled his chair around to face the window.

"Trouble follows you wherever you go, and from what Montana told me, it followed you to Savannah's. Stay away from her, and I mean it."

"Sir, I apologize if someone was following me. I have it under control and promise you that nothing will happen to her."

"Exactly. As of today all communication between her and you will cease."

"Sir, I mean no disrespect, but who I talk to on my own time is none of your business."

"It might not be, but Savannah is. She's like a daughter to me and I'll be damned if I let your line of work be the cause of her death, like Major's."

"Speaking of Major, have you gotten close to finding his killer?" Troy asked.

"No, I have no leads."

Troy thought it was odd that he didn't stay on top of his best friend's murder. He made a mental note about it. "It still tears me up that he was taken out like that," Troy said.

"Let me worry about that. You just worry about your security firm, and leave everything else to us."

"So you think his death is related to one of his previous assignments?"

"If I did know, I wouldn't tell you. If I didn't know any better, I would think you're up to more than what you're letting on."

"Sir, I'm just following up. My clients keep me busy, believe that."

"If there's nothing else, Relentless, I hope not to talk with you again."

When the phone clicked, Troy said, "I hope not either."

~ 12 ~

"It's done," Asia said, walking into the living room, where Savannah and Montana were sitting. Asia sat down on the floor near the coffee table. "Sorry, it took so long, but I had to make sure I didn't accidentally erase the contents."

Savannah placed the newspaper down. "I'll give Troy the original tomorrow."

"Speaking of Troy, don't you think he's fine with a capital F?" Asia asked.

Savannah responded, "He's all right."

"All right. Girl, you would have to be blind not to see how fine he is," Montana added.

"If you think that, go for it," Savannah responded, picking up the newspaper to hide her face.

Montana reached over and pulled down the paper. "Now, you know the golden rule is never to go after the man one of your sisters has an interest in."

Savannah put down the paper again and faced Asia. "I didn't know you were interested in Troy."

Asia threw a pillow at her. "Don't even try to play us. We see the looks."

Savannah feigned innocence. "I don't know what you're talking about."

The doorbell rang and interrupted the conversation. All made sure they would be ready just in case it was trouble at the door. Savannah looked through the peephole and said, "It's Uncle Raymond."

Montana frowned. "Sorry."

"Let me do most of the talking," Savannah said. "Put those away."

They put their guns in a nearby drawer.

"Uncle Raymond," Savannah said with enthusiasm, and a smile. Each sister took turns hugging him.

"Thought I would stop by and check on my favorite girls. I actually didn't expect to see you two," he said, looking between Montana and Asia.

Montana looped her arm through his. "We decided to have a girls' night."

"Do you want anything to drink?" Savannah asked.

"Some water. I'm trying to lay off the alcohol—doctor's orders."

Montana volunteered, "I'll get it." She left them in the living room.

Asia asked, "Is there something you haven't told us?"

He patted his chest. "This old man here is in perfect shape. Don't go writing my obituary yet."

Asia sat back down on the floor as their uncle Raymond took a seat in the chair.

"It's been a rough year," Asia commented.

"You girls are looking great, though. In spite of everything," he responded.

Savannah wanted to say something but decided to play it by ear. He didn't drop by at nine o'clock at night for a social visit. He would have called. One thing her dad taught her was never let anyone know everything.

After about fifteen minutes of small talk, Raymond Steel said, "Vanna, you need to make sure you don't get too involved with Troy. Your father would agree."

Savannah saw Asia open her mouth and she kicked her. Asia rubbed her leg. Savannah responded, "I know you mean well, but I can handle Troy."

"That's my point. You think you can. Did he tell you he got kicked out of The Agency?" The sisters looked at one another. "He wouldn't tell you. Trust me when I say, he can't be trusted."

"There's nothing to worry about."

Raymond didn't look convinced. "Call me if he contacts you again. He's up to something, and I don't want you girls getting involved."

"Uncle Raymond, we can take care of ourselves." Savannah tried not to sound irritated.

"And you, young lady. You need to let me handle this whole situation surrounding Major's death."

Montana stuttered, "I s—sort of overreacted. With the break-in I—I was just scared. I couldn't stand losing someone else I loved."

Savannah went and hugged her. "I'm not going anywhere."

"See, you girls are going to have me crying."

Asia said, "Sorry, Unc. As you can tell, we're just a little emotional right now."

Savannah sat back down in her seat. "This was our first year of not having Dad share in family events. So it's still a little rough for us. I just need some closure."

"I'll get you the closure. Just let me do my job."

"Do you have an idea who could have done it?"

"Not really. If I did, believe me they would be punished."

Savannah saw his eye twitch. She knew there was something he wasn't telling. She pretended to go along with him. She decided to fish for more information.

"In the report we read, it was labeled as a home invasion," Montana said.

Savannah added, "But nothing was taken. That seemed suspicious to me."

"True. But after I had my team investigate, it was determined that it had nothing to do with any of his past cases."

"Whew. That's a relief," Asia said.

Raymond shifted in his seat. "I didn't want to say anything, but with everything that's happened, I better." With all eyes on him Raymond said, "One of my sources is saying that Troy may know more about this, and that's why I'm concerned for your safety. If he's behind what happened to Major, your lives could be in danger."

"According to Troy, Dad was a good friend."

Raymond looked Savannah in the eye. "Everyone who professes to be your friend isn't. Be careful who it is you align your loyalty with."

A chill ran up Savannah's spine. A part of her reacted as if his words were more of a warning about himself than about Troy.

He looked at his watch. "Ladies, it's getting late. I need to be getting home. I have an early meeting in the morning. Savannah, walk me out."

Savannah followed him to the door. "Uncle Raymond, I didn't want to say this in front of my sisters, but I feel there's more to it all. What is it that you're not telling us?"

His eyes turned to a dark color. "In a situation like this, the less you know, the safer you are." He bent down and kissed her on the cheek.

Her body shivered as she watched him walk to his car. When he got to his door, he turned around and waved. She waved back. She closed the door and locked it.

"Ladies, we have a problem," she said as she walked back in the living room.

"Was it just me? Didn't he seem like he was hiding something?" Asia asked.

"He knows more than what he's saying, that's for sure. From this point forward, do not—and I repeat, do not—tell Uncle Raymond anything."

Asia and Savannah both turned and looked at Montana.

"What? Okay, so I made a mistake." Montana threw her hands up in the air.

"Calm down. That's the past. We can only deal with the here and now. It's late and we have a full day ahead of us," Savannah said.

Asia yawned. "I got second shift."

Montana said, "Since I opened my big mouth, I'll take the first shift. You two go on up. Asia, believe me, I'll be waking you up when it's your turn."

"No, Montana. I got first shift. Get some rest. Asia will be your relief."

"You sure?" she asked.

"Yes. Now y'all go before I change my mind." Savannah used her hands to shoo them away.

She checked the windows and doors before camping out in the living room. She watched a few reruns of her favorite show, *CSI*, until it was Asia's turn to take over.

"See you in the morning." Savannah left Asia downstairs and headed to her bedroom. She was asleep before her head hit the pillow. She kept having the same recurring dream. The person who killed her dad was now chasing after her. The killer's face was blank, but the laughter, the voice yelling out at her, sounded familiar.

Savannah woke up the next morning in a cold sweat.

~ *13* ~

"Rise and shine, sleepyhead," Savannah's voice resounded from the other end of the phone.

Troy's eyes remained closed. "What time is it?"

"It's eight. I just called to say there has been a change of plans. I'll meet you at your place."

"Uh. Give me a minute." He blinked his eyes a few times and then sat up in the bed. "You know how to get to the area, right?"

"Yes. I know that, but what street do I need to turn on?"

"Call me when you get in the area, and then I'll walk you through."

"Okay."

"Savannah?"

"Yes."

The thoughts running through his mind weren't pure. "Nothing. I'll talk to you when you get here."

As much as he wanted to roll back into the bed, he couldn't. After taking a long, hot shower, he got dressed and decided to cook breakfast. He forgot to ask her if she was hungry, but it didn't matter, because he was. Forty-five minutes later his phone rang again. He gave her step-by-step directions. A few minutes later she was ringing his doorbell.

Savannah hugged him when she walked through the door. Caught completely off guard by her show of emotions, Troy said, "I could stand to use another one of those."

"Only one hug allotment a day," she joked. She followed him to the kitchen. "All of this for me."

The skillet and pans were filled with bacon, eggs, grits, and biscuits. "I take it you're hungry."

"Yes. Montana was cooking when I left."

"It'll be ready in a few."

They joked over a hearty breakfast. After she cleaned up the table, Savannah reached into her purse and handed him an envelope. "I come bearing gifts."

"You've been holding out on me." He opened up the envelope containing a disc and a note.

Savannah said, "You had to feed me first."

"Follow me."

Troy led her to what he called his computer room. Before entering, however, he had to enter a code before the door would open.

"High-tech. I'm impressed."

"This may take a while."

"I have all day." Savannah pulled up a chair and sat beside him.

While he tried to decipher the codes, Savannah talked. He normally worked by himself, and it usually annoyed him when someone was invading his space. It surprised him that he liked her being there. He snapped out of his daze when he heard his ex-commander's name mentioned.

Savannah voiced, "To be honest, I probably shouldn't trust either one of you."

He stopped typing on the keyboards. "Good old Commander Steel never liked me, so I'm not surprised. I would try to convince you otherwise, but you're a grown woman and can make your own decision."

"Glad you recognized that."

Savannah seemed a little on the defensive. Troy didn't have time to pacify her, so he put his attention back on the computer screen. Now she was going on and on about her sisters. He stopped typing and faced her. "I don't mean to sound rude, but do you ever shut up?"

"Excuse me."

"You've been talking ever since you sat down. If you haven't noticed, I'm trying to crack this code. Your talking isn't helping me any."

"Fine." She stood up and pushed the chair away. "I'll take a look around your castle."

Troy felt a little guilty for purposely starting the little disagreement, but he could no longer concentrate with her there. He could deal with the talking, but Savannah's exotic perfume was getting to him, getting his mind to wandering, when he needed all of his brain cells to concentrate on the matter at hand.

Major made his job hard, but he knew why. The disc in the wrong hands could be deadly. He cracked the code and was in the process of deciphering the document, when he heard Savannah scream.

He grabbed his gun out of the drawer and ran toward the sound of her voice. He almost laughed when he saw her standing on the bed. He put the gun in his back pocket.

"Why didn't you tell me you had a pet snake?" she yelled.

"You never asked." He laughed.

Savannah threw the pillows at him.

"I'm keeping it for a friend. I didn't expect your nosy behind to venture into this guest room."

Savannah got off the bed and walked close to the edge until she got to the door. "Of course you wouldn't mention it. Snakes protect each other."

He giggled as he followed her out of the room. He closed the door. "My guest will be leaving next week."

"Well, you don't have to worry about me. As soon as you tell me what's on that disc, I'm leaving."

"Get ready to camp out. This is going to be an all-day thing," Troy responded.

"Hop to it. Why are you wasting time?"

"Need I remind you that I came to rescue you? How soon we forget."

Savannah opened her mouth to speak. Troy interrupted her before she could say anything. "No. Just stay out of that room. In fact, why don't you go home and I'll call you when I'm through."

"Not. But I will check on my sisters." She followed him back to his computer room. She called her sisters on her cell phone as he worked. When he would look up, she was watching him. She would pretend not to and then go back to talking on the phone.

"Bingo!" he said out loud.

"Got to go," Savannah said, and flipped her phone off.

She got up from the chair and stood behind him. She leaned down and the scent of her perfume attacked his nostrils. It wasn't the fact that her perfume was strong, but with her being in such close proximity, her scent excited not only his senses, but also his male organ.

"Seems like your uncle Raymond is more involved than he wants anyone to know."

~ *14* ~

Savannah pulled up a chair next to Troy's desk and asked excitedly, "What do you mean?"

"According to your dad's notes, he's behind this outfit of men who are vigilantes."

"That's the same thing he accuses you of being."

"Exactly. I've never been a vigilante. I'm about justice and seeing that it's served. Granted, some folks got killed in the process, but it's not because of my doing."

"I don't know what to believe anymore," Savannah said as she looked away.

"It's here." He turned the monitor around to show her what her dad had written.

"This can't be. He's been like an uncle to me and to my sisters. It's going to break their hearts."

"Hold up. It doesn't say he killed your dad."

"Might as well. If he's in cahoots with them, he's just as guilty."

Troy could see the pain on her face. He wished he could erase it, but he wasn't so sure of Raymond's innocence himself.

"He was just at my house. He swore he would get to the bottom of this. He said he was going to help." Savannah went on and on with her monologue.

Troy allowed her this time to vent. He knew how it felt to be betrayed. She would have to deal with this type of betrayal on her own, but he would be there to help in any way he could. First by making sure Raymond paid for his part in Major's death.

"I still have some more to decipher, so maybe we're both overreacting," he said.

"My instincts tell me we're not," Savannah said, sounding defeated. "I need a drink."

"Soda is in the fridge," he responded.

"I got it. Just continue to work on that disc," Savannah said, leaving him to his thoughts.

Savannah paced the floor back and forth while nursing the soda in her right hand. Her mind tried to grasp all that she had learned about Uncle Raymond. Her father taught her to trust her instincts, and from the beginning she didn't trust him enough to go to him about her suspicions. She was livid. He had just left her house the night before, and had acted all concerned. She recalled the last thing he said to her, and now it all made sense. He was threatening her. How could he? She wanted to yell, but she didn't want Troy to think she was a basket case. One scream a day was enough.

Regardless of what else Troy might discover, things with Uncle Raymond would never be the same. She suspected he knew exactly who had killed her dad, and he wasn't doing a thing about it. He would pay just like the rest of them. How or when wasn't important, but he would pay.

Finding her father's killer kept her from falling into a depressed state of mind. Nobody knew—not even her sisters—how she suffered with the same recurring nightmare of finding her father and holding him in her arms before he took his last breath. She didn't have the dream every night—well, now she didn't—but she still had the dream. It shook her core each time.

She was in deep thought, when she felt his presence. "I'm okay. Just admiring your garden."

"Gardening relaxes me. Reminds me of God's omnipresence," Troy responded.

"That's the same thing Dad used to say."

"My adopted mother used to garden. She tried to teach me, but I thought it was girl stuff, until one day I was having a conversation with Major about it. When I bought this house, planting a garden was one of the first things I did."

"He would be impressed," Savannah said.

"He was," Troy said with pride.

Savannah turned and faced him. "I take it you're through."

"For now. I wanted to check on you. I know you've had a lot to think about."

She crossed her arms and leaned on the counter. "Remember, I'm a big girl."

"Even big girls need a shoulder to lean on every now and then."

Before she could protest, he wrapped his arms around her. She leaned into his shoulder and embraced him.

She removed herself from his arms. She pretended to wipe off her clothes. "Enough of this mushy stuff. Show me what you got."

"You sure? Because I've been told I'm working with a lot."

She blushed. She recalled not only that he was well endowed, but he also had skills that made her have multiple orgasms. "I'm talking about the disc, silly."

"I didn't know. I thought it was time for big daddy to make its debut."

"Uh, no." She walked toward the computer room with Troy behind her.

She sat in his seat at the computer. He turned the chair around and sat down. He scrolled the screen down, showing her some other things he had discovered.

"Your dad was the best. This is a list of men who are double agents. Your dad loved The Agency, and he loved his country. Scroll down here." He gave Savannah a chance to read over it before continuing. "He was about to expose them. From his notes he had confided in the commander."

Savannah completed his statement by reading what was on the screen. Savannah heard her father's voice in her head as she read his words silently:

I never thought I would see the day that an agency to which I dedicated my life would have men in charge doing everything opposite of what we are to uphold. The integrity of The Agency was compromised the moment Raymond gave these men free rein to kill. I cannot, in good conscience, let this sort of practice continue. I'm at a crossroads because Raymond is not only a colleague, but also a friend. The talks I had with Raymond have not helped. He refused to redeem himself and stop these ill practices. I have no choice but to turn over this information to the Justice Department. If, by chance, someone else is reading this, then it means that I'm no longer here. Please make sure that you deliver this by hand to . . .

Savannah stopped reading and looked at Troy.

"I still have other things to decipher," he said.

"Thank you."

"I don't know how to say this, but I can't just hand this over to the Justice Department."

Savannah looked back at the computer. "Everything is here. Turn this in. They arrest the folks on the list, and one of them or several of them will be my dad's killer."

"My dear Savannah, if only it were that easy."

Savannah was confused. "What? You can't figure out the rest of the code."

Troy patted her hand. "If I hand this to the Justice Department now, you will never see your father's killer caught. The government takes care of its own. The fact your uncle knew about this is scary."

"It explains why he doesn't want me to have anything to do with you too."

"He just doesn't like me."

"No, but he said some other stuff that I didn't tell you." Savannah repeated some of the things he had said about Troy.

Troy's face turned red. He was livid. "He's on the top of my list to bring down."

"So what do we do next, since turning this over to the Justice Department isn't the right move?" Savannah leaned back in her chair.

"Oh, we're going to turn all of this in, but not before we finish what we started. You will get justice."

She kissed him on the cheek. "Thanks."

Troy's gesture of putting his hand to his face softened her heart. He winked. "Next time, Savannah, aim for the lips."

She playfully hit his lower arm.

He pulled it back. "Ouch. That's the same arm you twisted behind my back."

"You wimp."

"I got your wimp."

Troy tickled her and she giggled. They both hit the floor, laughing. The ringing of Savannah's cell phone interrupted their playtime.

"Hey, that's Montana. I got to get it." She rushed to get her phone and listened as her sister spoke. "We'll be right there." She disconnected and turned to Troy. "The rest of the disc will have to wait. Someone tried to break in again, but the intruder was stupid enough to come alone. Asia has the unwelcomed guest tied up."

"Let's go." Troy logged off and placed the disc in a protective covering. He slipped the disc in a secret compartment.

"Never would have thought to hide it under the lamp."

"And you thought I was just fashion conscious."

Savannah rushed to the door. "I'm not going to entertain you with a response."

Troy decided to ride with Savannah. Savannah sped through traffic and ran a few yellow lights to make it to her neighborhood in record time. "Stop here. That car looks out of place. I'll meet you back at your house," Troy said.

Once he got out, she sped down the street to her house. She didn't bother to park in the garage. Montana must have been watching for her, because she had the door opened before Savannah could insert her key.

"Where is he?" Savannah asked.

Savannah followed Montana into the downstairs guest bedroom. "There's something you should know," Montana said.

Before Montana could finish, Savannah had opened the door. She was expecting to see one of the men in black, but she was shocked to see whom Asia had tied up. She walked and stood in front of the person. Staring back at her, with a smug look on her face, was a woman with curly auburn hair. If they had been looking in a mirror together, she would have sworn she was looking at a relative, except they were of two different races.

"Scary, isn't it?" Asia said.

"Indeed" was all Savannah managed to say.

"She won't talk, but, you know, I could do like I see in the movies and rough her up a little," Asia said.

"That won't be necessary. Then again, if she doesn't tell me what she's doing here, I might just let you."

Savannah plopped on the bed right beside the intruder. "When I take the tape off your mouth, I want to know who you are and why you're here."

Savannah reached over to remove the tape. The intruder tried to bite her. Savannah slapped her mouth. "Let's try this again. Who are you and why are you here?"

In a monotone voice she responded, "Who I am isn't important. If I don't report back by a certain time, all of y'all can hang it up." Her laugh was sinister.

15

Troy waited for someone to come to the door. If they didn't hurry up, he would find another way in. Montana answered.

"Where are they?" he asked.

"I'm glad you're here. Maybe you can get her to talk," Montana said as she led him into a downstairs room.

When he arrived in the room, he saw Savannah slap the intruder. When he walked around to get a good look at the home invader, he knew exactly who she was. "We meet again," Troy said.

Savannah and her sisters looked at one another. Savannah was the first to speak. "You know her?"

"He knows all about me. Don't you, playboy?" She winked her eye.

Savannah crossed her arms. Troy tried to ease the tense situation. "Irene and I worked on a case together, but she switched teams."

"I work for the highest bidder."

"This reunion is fine and dandy, but let's save the small talk for later. Answer the lady. What are you doing here?"

"Steel underestimated you. You've been hanging out with his little girl." Irene looked at the three sisters. "You know that's what he calls you." She paused before continuing. "He thought Major left something here that belonged to The Agency. I came to retrieve it."

"So your orders were to retrieve some documents, and what else?" Troy asked.

"Now, Relentless . . . I mean Troy, you know my role."

Troy laughed. "He sends in the Terminator. He must be really scared." He looked at Savannah. "I got this. I think your sisters need your attention."

Savannah looked at the confused looks on their faces. "Y'all come on. I'll explain everything."

"You made a mistake by taking on this assignment."

She stood up and got closer to him. "I could cut you in, if you like. You already got them trusting you. Get me the documents, and I promise you'll be paid nicely."

He pushed her back on the bed. "You must think I'm a fool."

She fell back before catching her balance. "I heard you had your own security firm, and you do what others can't."

"I run a legitimate business. I don't go around killing innocent citizens."

Irene stared at him with contempt. "There aren't any cameras around. You can stop the act."

It took all of the restraint Troy could muster not to reach down and wrap his arms around her neck. She almost cost him his life a few years back, and he had wondered what he would do if he ever saw her again. He fell for her once, but never again.

"You got sixty seconds to tell me what document you're looking for."

"Or what? You're going to kill me," Irene said.

Savannah walked back in the room with her gun pointed. "No, but I might."

"Don't trust him, girl."

Troy went over to the bed and shook her. "I'm tired of playing."

Irene started laughing hysterically. Unbeknownst to Troy, Irene had maneuvered her hands free. She reached for Troy's gun. Savannah shot her before she could get to it. Irene screamed and doubled over. "She shot me. I can't believe she shot me." Blood oozed down her arm.

Troy pushed her farther on the bed. "As you can tell, we're not playing."

"Spoilsport. Major supposedly had a disc with some information that Steel wants."

"Call him." Troy removed a phone from his pocket and threw it to her.

"What am I going to say? Your crazy goddaughter shot me, and, by the way, Troy's still trouble."

Savannah waved the gun back and forth in the air. "I'm warning you. You say one more thing and I won't hesitate to shoot you again."

Troy looked at Savannah and then at Irene. "I wouldn't try her if I were you. My arm is still hurting from the last time we got into it."

Irene did as Troy directed. She threw the phone on the bed and said, "Troy, you forgot one of the rules. I'm the Terminator. I go out just the way I came in."

"Not this time, Irene." He looked at Savannah and said, "I think you might want to leave the room."

"What are you going to do?"

"I'm going to take care of our little problem."

"Troy, I was just kidding about killing her."

He pulled Savannah to the side. "If we let her go, you best believe Steel is going to send in some more arsenals. I can make her disappear. Her car is up the road. I need your sister's truck. Can you have her bring it to the garage?"

"Sure." Savannah didn't sound too convinced of his plan.

"They'll figure it out, and when they do, they'll come get you and your sisters!" Irene yelled at Savannah.

Troy knocked her out with one punch. "I normally don't hit women, but she's not a woman—she's a beast."

"Remind me not to make you mad," Savannah joked.

Troy tied Irene's arms and legs with some rope provided to him by Asia. This time he would make sure the knots were tight enough so she wouldn't be able to loosen them. He picked Irene up and threw her over his shoulder.

"Is all clear?" he asked Asia before leaving the room.

"What are you going to do with her?" she asked.

"It's best you don't know."

He went to the garage and placed her in the backseat of Montana's navy blue SUV. "I'll be back in about an hour or two."

Savannah jumped in the passenger seat. "I'm going with you."

"Your sisters need you."

Montana said, "We got this taken care of. In fact, why don't you get in the backseat? Just in case one of the neighbors is looking, it's best that Savannah drives."

Troy thought about it. "You're actually right. Don't answer the phone. Here." He handed Montana a cell phone. "This line is untraceable. You already have my number, so call me on it if you need either one of us. Savannah, where's your phone?"

"Right here," she responded.

"I need it."

Savannah handed him the phone. He, in turn, handed it to Montana. "I'll get more phones like this. Irene showing up here turns things up a notch. You two . . . be careful. Come on, we don't have much time."

He switched seats with Savannah. He leaned his seat back so if anyone was looking, the neighbor wouldn't be able to tell if someone else was in the SUV. When they made it to the end of the street, Troy pulled up his seat. He pulled out his cell phone. He gave directions to one of his workers.

"Slow down," he said to Savannah.

"The sooner we unload our passenger, the better I'll feel."

Troy gave Savannah directions. Savannah kept her eyes peeled on the road. Troy took her through many curves and turns. The road went from a regular highway to a dirt road. They pulled up to what appeared to be a modern-day fortress. A guard walked to Savannah's window.

"Ma'am, may I help you? Oh, boss, I didn't see you," the big, burly guy said as he waved his hand at Troy.

"She's cool," Troy said. "We're delivering a package."

The guard pressed a button and the gate opened.

"I don't know what to say," Savannah said.

Troy hoped he hadn't made a bad decision bringing Savannah to his secret haven. If he had, it was too late now. He removed Irene from the car and instructed Savannah to remain behind. After taking Irene inside and giving instructions to his men, Troy returned to the truck. "Let's roll."

Savannah remembered how to get home without any assistance from Troy. On the ride back Savannah didn't ask any questions, and Troy didn't give any answers.

16

Savannah parked Montana's SUV in the garage. "I want to ask you something before we go back in." Savannah reached for Troy's arm before he could exit the passenger side.

"Ask away."

"What's going to happen to her?"

Troy waited a few seconds before responding. "If she's good, she'll be contained until this whole mess is over. If she's bad—let's just say—we have ways to deal with her."

"Say no more." Savannah exited the vehicle. She used her key to gain entry into the house.

Asia was on the couch sleeping and Montana was on her laptop typing. "I was just about to call you," Montana said after glancing at the clock.

"All is well," Savannah said. "Anybody hungry? I can whip us up something real quick."

"How can you eat? My stomach is still in knots," Montana commented.

Troy intervened. "Why don't you rest up and let me do the cooking."

Savannah looked at him. "Oh, you're a regular Chef Boyardee."

"Being a bachelor, if I didn't cook for myself, I would starve."

"And it's obvious you're not starving," Asia sluggishly said.

"You can go back to sleep," Troy joked.

Asia sat up on the couch and yawned. Once Troy was out of the room, she asked, "So what happened?"

Savannah looked to make sure Troy wasn't coming back. She gave them a condensed version. She didn't mention where they took her, because of her promise to Troy. "Asia, I have to say, I'm proud of how you handled our unwanted guest."

Asia blew on her knuckles. "I might not be as in shape as you two, but I still work out every now and then."

"Speaking of working out, I haven't asked him yet, but I will. Troy trains people to do undercover operations. We need to brush up on some skills, and he's the perfect person to help us."

Montana closed her laptop. "I found some stuff that we need, so I'll be going by to pick it up tomorrow. I took a leave of absence, but they are expecting me back in about four weeks."

"Well, that means we need to get busy. What about your job, Asia?"

"They screamed, but I told them my family is important and I needed to take care of you until you could get back on your feet."

"As long as they bought it."

Montana shook her head from side to side. "I'm still trying to grasp how Uncle Raymond could betray us . . . and Dad the way that he has."

"Money will do it to you," Asia said.

"I don't know if it was greed or an ego thing, but he'll go down, just like the rest of them. The only loyalty I have is to you two," Savannah said.

"What about Troy?" Montana asked.

"What about him? Dad is the only man I trusted. Troy is a matter of convenience. Once he's helped us with this, his services will no longer be needed."

"Yeah, right," Asia said before winking her eye in Montana's direction.

"Sis, it's us. We know you," Montana said.

"I know me too, so, anyway, back to what's important. Troy was able to decipher some of the message on the disc, so we have a list of people whom we need to find out more about." She looked at Asia. "I want you to work with him so you can get as much information as you can about each person on the list. I think I recall seeing that Irene person's name on the list, so that's one down."

"We need a game plan. After Asia does that, what's next?" Montana asked.

"Let me think on it. I need to talk to Troy about some stuff first." Savannah never thought her project-management skills would be used to plan a mission that would hopefully result in justice for her dad's killer or killers.

Asia held her arm out with a balled-out fist. "To the Blake sisters."

Savannah and Montana did the same. They repeated it several times. Savannah left them in the living room and followed the aroma of spices to the kitchen. She stopped in the doorway of the kitchen and watched Troy place the casserole dish in the oven.

"I hope it's not too spicy," he said, turning in her direction.

"We're Louisiana girls, the spicier the better." She sat at the kitchen table and watched him cut potatoes.

"Do you want something?" Troy asked.

"No, I just like looking at you." Savannah smiled.

"I'm glad you're amused."

Savannah said, "I need you to put us through your training, but the accelerated course."

Troy stopped cutting and looked at Savannah. "I got trained men who can handle this."

"I'm not hiring you."

"Didn't ask you to."

Savannah pulled her cell phone out of her pocket. "If you don't help, then I'll just find someone else who will." The kind of training they were looking for could not be found by looking through the Yellow Pages of the phone book. She hoped Troy didn't call her bluff.

"What exactly do you need?" Troy asked while chopping the potatoes and putting them in a boiler.

Savannah wondered if he was thinking about her the way he was destroying those potatoes.

"Teach us more defensive moves. We used to work out with Dad when he would be in town, and more when he retired. I slacked off when he died."

"I can do that."

"Put us through the scenario training that you put your workers through."

"I'll have to think on that."

"Troy, it's a must. We're going to be faced with more dangerous situations, and I need to know that we can handle ourselves. All of us have black belts, but there are some other things you can teach us."

Troy rubbed his arm. "If they have moves like you, they'll be all right." His dimples got bigger as he smiled.

"It'll teach you for sneaking up on someone. But seriously, we could all use some more moves."

"Got you."

"We also need to know about gadgets?"

"Gadgets?"

"You know, spyware, and I'm not talking about the spyware on the computer."

Troy took a seat across from Savannah. "I guess I can help you with that too."

"Wow. Thanks for the favor."

"Anytime." Troy leaned back in his chair.

"If I didn't need you, I would hurt that other arm."

"I'm going to make sure you and I spar together, trust me."

"I look forward to it." She couldn't stop smiling. "Also, I wasn't going to say anything, but Asia is a computer whiz. Work with her on the list."

"She might be a whiz, but there are things on there that even I have a hard time deciphering."

"Dad taught her some things, and she'll be more useful than you think."

Troy looked to be in deep thought. "I'll think about it."

Savannah pulled away from the table. "Do that."

"Vanna, you're something else." He knew she hadn't given him permission to use her nickname, but it was the cleanest nickname he could think of at this time. He had to get a grip on his libido, because she was getting under his skin. Although Troy didn't want to admit it, Savannah was also tugging at his heart. Before she could protest, Troy pulled her into an embrace.

17

Troy enjoyed watching the sisters interact with one another. Training these three ladies would indeed be a challenge. If it meant being around Savannah, he would be up for the challenge. While they cleaned up the kitchen after dinner, he made a few phone calls.

They were giggling but stopped when he reentered the kitchen. He knew from their expression that they had been talking about him. "We're all set. You ladies should meet me at my office at zero eight hundred."

"Cool. I can't wait." Asia was the first to speak.

"It's getting late and we have a full day ahead of us. I'll see you all in the morning," Troy said before turning to walk out.

He heard Montana say, "Walk him out."

He slowed his pace so Savannah could catch up with him. "You have to ignore my sisters," she said as they reached the door.

Troy turned around to face her. "I look forward to sparring with you tomorrow."

"You better go home and practice, because I have a few surprise moves I've been saving just for the occasion."

He kissed her on the forehead and left. He waved at her as she watched him from the doorway.

The next morning Troy woke up a few hours early so he could get to the office before Savannah and her sisters. He briefed his staff on his new clients; he still did not give them details on their ties to The Agency. He called Savannah and informed her of the alias names they were to use when checking into the premises. He stressed the importance of them using the pseudonyms.

"Your code name is Diamond. Asia is Foxy and Montana is Red."

When his assistant walked the three sisters in, he had to do a double take because each had changed her appearance. He could still tell they were the Blake sisters, but the slight change was enough to make him smile. These sisters meant business. They were dressed to train.

"You can thank Montana for this transformation," Savannah said.

"If you need a job, I could always use your services," Troy addressed Montana.

She ran her hand through her now auburn ponytail. "That's okay. I'll stick with my day job."

They were all dressed in sweatpants and looked eager to get started.

"Follow me." Troy led them to a building that appeared to be a warehouse from the outside, but on the inside had state-of-the-art tactical equipment. "Mike, take these two to the range. Start off light. By the end of the day I want to see them going through course five."

"Course five. Sir, I don't think . . ." He looked at Montana and Asia and stopped in midsentence. If looks could kill, he would be mincemeat. "Are you sure?"

"You tell me. See you at the end of the day." He addressed Montana and Asia. "If you need anything, call me. Otherwise, Mike will be your guide for the day."

"What about her?" Montana asked.

"I got other plans for Ms. Lady."

"I'm sure you do," Asia said.

Troy laughed as he watched Mike take Asia and Montana away. He knew Mike had his hands full, and he didn't envy him at all. The expression on Savannah's face when he turned around made him want to switch places with Mike.

"You all have it bad, talking about me like I'm not there," she snapped.

"Hold on to that attitude. You'll need it during our sparring session."

Troy had fun teasing Savannah. "Put these on." He handed her a pair of gloves where her fingers stuck out of the end. While she was putting her gloves on, Troy said, "Pretend I'm an attacker. How would you respond when I did this?" Before she could react, Troy was behind her and had her neck under his arm. "No kicking in the groin either—well, unless absolutely necessary."

Savannah tried her best to loosen herself from his grip but was unable to do so. He held on to her tighter than he probably should have, but he knew if she was in a real situation, the attacker wouldn't be easy on her.

"I know you already know this, but use your heel," Troy said. "Remember, you can pretty much gauge the height of your attacker from how far his or her waist is on your back. Use your heel and kick the area of the leg with all your might. If hit, the attacker will loosen his grip."

"Like this?" Savannah tried the move. Troy loosened his grip.

"Yeah, but did you have to hit so hard?" he teased.

"Just trying to keep it real," she responded.

"Next move. Sit down at the table."

Savannah followed his directions. She sat and pretended to be reading the magazine.

"Always be aware of your surroundings. If anyone is watching you, they're hoping to catch you off guard.

They could care less if you're in a crowded place or if
you're by yourself." Troy picked up a few items and
said, "I want you to use your peripheral vision and tell
me what you see."

He was impressed with how Savannah was able to
name a few things. She missed a few, but that was to be
expected. "How did I do?" she asked.

"Fine for a first timer," he responded.

She turned around. "I think I did darn well. I got everything right except for those two."

"We're going to do this exercise again until it's one
hundred percent."

Savannah rolled her eyes but turned around; they
practiced until she was able to do it without an error.

"Satisfied," she said, pulling away from the table.

He licked his lips. "Very."

"You're a sexist."

He batted his eyes. "My feelings are hurt."

"I don't have time to play with you. What's next?"
she asked. Although Savannah pretended to be upset,
Troy could tell she wasn't. He admired her eagerness.

"Show me some of those black-belt moves," he said.
He led her onto a huge black mat.

She stood at a stance. "I'll be happy to."

Neither used full force when sparring with each
other. "Not bad," he said.

She knocked him off his feet. "Sorry." She folded her
arms and smiled.

He bounced back up. "Oh, you want to play dirty.
Bring it on."

For the next thirty minutes they continued to hit
each other and pick each other up. He dusted himself
off.

"I don't know about you, but I could use a break,"
Savannah said.

"Giving up, are we?" he joked.

"Never."

"Come on." He handed her a towel. "You can freshen up in there and I'll meet you back out here in a few."

Troy went to the small refrigerator in the corner and retrieved a couple of bottles of water and sports drinks. He removed two small bags of trail mix from the cabinet. He was drinking water when Savannah returned.

She sat next to him and gulped down the water.

"That was not ladylike," he joked.

She threw up her middle finger. "Take that."

"Only if you're willing to give it," he responded.

They shared a quiet break, drinking and eating the snacks.

"You don't have to push yourself so hard, you know," Troy said while waiting for her to finish her snack.

"I can't afford to be slack either," she said in between bites. "I wonder how my sisters are doing."

"We could actually see from my makeshift office over there."

Savannah followed him as he turned on the monitor. Savannah commented, "Looks like they're doing pretty good to me. Let me check on something."

Troy called Mike. "How's their score?" He paused. "Need to get it up to ninety and then move on to the next phase." He hung up with Mike and said, "You ladies are better than what I thought. You are doing things that it takes some folks months to learn."

"We're the Blake sisters. Come on now." Savannah winked her right eye.

~ *18* ~

Savannah's entire body was hurting by the time she and her sisters made it back home. Each sister seemed to be deep in thought, because the ride home was quiet.

"I don't know about y'all, but I'm about to take me a long, hot bath," Savannah said, rubbing her thighs.

"My arms are tired, but that's about it," said Asia. She did a few arm exercises to ease the tension in her muscles.

"I don't know if I'm cut out for this," Montana added.

"No backing out now," Asia said.

"Montana, you have to. When I send you undercover, I need to feel confident that you can handle yourself, or else our plans won't work."

Montana crossed her arms. "Maybe if you shared some details, it would encourage me to continue with this torture."

"I'm still figuring it out in my head. But by the time we're through with the training, we will all sit down and map everything out," Savannah responded.

She left Asia teasing Montana, and she was relieved to hear Montana say, "There's no way I'm letting you outdo me."

Savannah said out loud, "Way to go, Asia." She would have to thank Asia privately for engaging Montana in a competition. Now she felt better. She needed all three of them to be fit and capable. At least she could have that peace of mind.

The water felt soothing as she eased her body into the suds. *"Aweee."* Savannah leaned her head back onto the towel she had on the back of the tub and closed her eyes. She allowed the hot water to soak her skin. As the temperature of the water dropped, Savannah washed and rubbed various body parts to ease the tension.

Refreshed, but still a little sore, she got out of the tub and toweled herself dry. Her mind went back to her sparring sessions with Troy. Under normal circumstances it would have been fun working up a sweat with him. He was patient with her, even when she knew her tough-girl exterior was a little over-the-top. She didn't want to admit it, but he did mean more to her than she would admit to him or her sisters. For now, she would keep her developing feelings for Troy a secret. She had one mission, and falling back in love with Troy wasn't it.

"I've worked up an appetite," Savannah said after she dressed and strolled downstairs.

"Who is taking first shift tonight?" Asia asked.

"I got the whole night. You two sleep well. You're going to need your energy," Savannah responded.

"That's not fair," Montana said.

"I can still get some sleep. Besides, I sleep lighter than you two. I'll just camp out downstairs, and if anything happens, I'll yell."

They shared the events of the day over a light dinner of soup and a sandwich. Instead of staying up late talking, like they had been doing, Montana and Asia retired upstairs early to get a head start on the next day. It didn't take Savannah long to fall asleep either.

The sun was beaming the next time Savannah's eyes opened. To her relief she had a peaceful night. No strange noises and no nightmares. She showered and got dressed. She wanted to surprise her sisters with a hearty breakfast, but the refrigerator was bare. Instead, she made a huge pot of oatmeal, something that would stick to the bones and be filling. She thought back to the times her mom would cook oatmeal in the mornings for her and Montana before they went to school. She wasn't sad at all. She smiled remembering better times.

Montana entered the kitchen. "Ooh, my favorite." She headed straight to the stove and lifted the top off the pot.

"I need to do some grocery shopping, so that's all I've got." Savannah poured herself some apple juice.

"I'm serious. It's hard making a good batch of oatmeal. Yours reminds me of mom's." Montana grabbed a bowl and filled it up with oatmeal.

She was eating before Asia entered. "I'll take a bowl of that."

"Is this the Twilight Zone?" Savannah asked.

"What do you mean?" Asia asked.

"Both of you come in here all cheery-eyed and jolly. Pinch me, I must be dreaming."

Montana stretched. "A good night's sleep will do it to you."

After breakfast they headed to the training facilities. Troy wasn't there, but he had left detailed training instructions with his employees. Savannah went to the firing range, while her sisters did more of a physical training with Mike and a new guy.

During her course of firearms training, Savannah pictured the target as Uncle Raymond. In her mind, whether he pulled the trigger that killed her dad or not, Raymond could have stopped it from possibly happening. Did Raymond feel threatened by her father? Did he think her dad would turn him in, so he had one of his men take him out?

There were so many questions, and no answers. At this point Raymond had no clue the Blake sisters were on to him. Savannah couldn't let her anger play her hand, until it was time. Instead, with each pull of the trigger, she released the anger she had. The love she once had for Uncle Raymond had turned to hate. She just hoped she could release the hate so it wouldn't eat at her like the pain of losing her dad had done. Now she'd lost two important men in her life.

"That's my girl," Troy said as he clapped.

"Glad I could make you proud." Savannah shot the last few rounds of her gun.

Troy pulled the target closer. "Bull's-eye every time."

Savannah shaped her hand like a gun and blew on the tip of her finger. "Every time."

"Sorry, I'm late, but I spent last night deciphering the rest of the letter."

"I told you Asia could help you with that."

"I got another assignment for Asia."

Savannah followed Troy out of the range and into his office. He turned on his laptop and showed Savannah the rest of the information on the disc. She tapped her fingers on the desk out of habit. The more she read, the louder her taps got. Troy reached out and placed his hand over hers.

"Man, what have I gotten us into?" Savannah threw her hand over her face.

Troy moved her hands. "I like the fact that you're not trying to be a victim. You're taking control, and that's where your enemies will be at a disadvantage." He paused. "That, and the fact you can kick butt."

"What about the gear? I need some state-of-the-art stuff. Not that junk you get from the galleria, and it only works half the time."

"Already on it. I'll wait until your sisters are ready and I'll show you all at the same time."

"So what are your plans for me today?"

"I'll let you choose. What do you feel like you need to practice?"

Savannah felt a magnetic pull toward Troy. Not one to be bashful, she said, "I need this." Before he could respond, Savannah leaned over and kissed him. She tried to remain in control, but Troy took over from there. Their tongues danced with one another. He pulled her onto his lap. Neither would surrender to the other; yet neither would stop kissing.

Troy's ringing phone broke them out of the trance. Savannah jumped up from his lap and wiped her mouth. "I shouldn't have." She ran toward the door.

"Wait."

"No, I need some space," she responded. She didn't wait for him to reply. His assistant looked at her strangely. She didn't stop. She recalled passing a bathroom on the way up, so she headed toward it. Once there, she took some cold water and washed her face. She looked at her reflection in the mirror. She was just emotional right now. The combination of her emotions and adrenaline explained why she had kissed him. She paced back and forth in front of the mirror. How could she face him after that? She didn't want him to get the wrong idea. The past needed to stay in the past. Rekindling a love affair with Troy spelled disaster. She let out a few deep breaths. She stood up straight and walked back to his office. She closed the door and sat and waited patiently for him to get off the phone. She pretended to be reading a magazine.

She heard him say, "Get it to me by the end of the day tomorrow or you can cancel the rest of those orders." Troy slammed the phone down.

"Problems?" She threw the magazine on the top of his desk.

"Nothing that I can't handle," he responded. "We need to talk."

"Save it for another time. We have more important things to discuss."

Troy leaned back in his chair. They stared at each other for a few minutes. "Fine. Suit yourself. This isn't the last of this. In fact, we're just getting started."

"Let's pretend like it didn't happen," Savannah said.

"Do you really think we can do that?" Troy asked.

Fortunately, before Savannah had a chance to respond, they were interrupted by his assistant's knock on the door.

~ *19* ~

Troy could sense Savannah's relief when Cheryl walked through the door.

Cheryl said, "I need your signature on these." She looked at the two of them as if she knew she interrupted something. She didn't say anything, but the smile on her face was a dead giveaway. She winked at him as she backed out the door.

Troy made a mental note to talk to her before the day was out to make sure she didn't start any false rumors. His employees were trusted individuals, but since they were a close-knit group, the ones in the office could intrude on one another's personal turf. He didn't mind at all, because it made him feel like being part of a family. In fact, most of them didn't grow up within a traditional family structure. They either grew up in single-parent households or were orphans like himself.

Right now, he had to deal with Ms. Savannah. She was ignoring their attraction, and it was fine for now. Eventually, though, it would be something they both would have to face. She surprised him with her kiss, but he would not let her catch him off guard again.

He watched her pretend to be interested in the magazine she was reading. It would have helped if the magazine had been upright, instead of upside down. He chuckled.

"What's so funny?" she asked.

"Come on. Time to get busy. You've goofed around long enough." He grabbed his keys and walked toward the door. He loved to get her riled up. In his opinion it made her sexier, if that were even possible.

He led her through a maze and they ended up in the basement of the building. "What you're about to see is highly confidential. I won't be bringing your sisters here."

The room was filled with three men and two women, who were monitoring computer screens and manning telephones.

"This is how I keep in contact with my men in the field."

"Everyone, this is Diamond. She's a new recruit. She'll be working with me on a special case."

They all spoke. Savannah almost forgot her alias.

He pushed a button on a keyboard and scrolled down. "We keep track of their location, and if anything happens out of the ordinary, we have people in various places."

Savannah concentrated on the screen. He turned the screen off. Troy said, "Come on." He entered a code and the door clicked and allowed them entrance into another room.

"This is where we keep secret documents."

Savannah asked, "Why are you showing me all of this?"

"Because I want to prove to you that we're a team. I have no secrets." He had one, but he wasn't ready to reveal his feelings for her.

"I'm satisfied."

"I aim to please."

He showed her a few more sensitive spots before heading to the warehouse, where they had trained yesterday. "Let's check on your sisters and then get a few more rounds in ourselves," he said.

"You sure you want more of this?" Savannah teased.

"I'm just getting started."

"Hi, ladies," Troy said when they entered the section where Montana and Asia were training. He addressed Mike. "How are they doing?"

"You should have warned me. My back's a little sore from that one." Mike pointed to Asia.

Troy patted him on the shoulder. "You'll be all right."

"Tell that to her," Mike said before he returned to where Asia was standing.

"Let's do a few rounds in the ring," Troy challenged Savannah.

"I don't box," Savannah responded.

"I can teach you."

After a few minutes of thinking about it, Savannah said, "Be gentle."

"Always."

Each of the sisters did different workouts with Troy and his men. Savannah was worn-out after her boxing match with Troy. Troy let her get a few jabs in to build up her confidence. This exercise was more to build up her stamina than anything else. He was confident that she could knock out someone if the situation arose.

Troy sensed exhaustion with all three sisters. "Let's call it a day," he said. "Instead of meeting here, though, I would like for you all to come to my house tomorrow."

"I'm all for that," Savannah responded in between taking sips of water.

"Let's wrap it up," Troy said out loud to everyone else.

"Good, because I was tired of beating his butt," Asia teased.

Mike grunted. "Boss, I'll talk to you later." The look he gave Asia had everyone laughing. "Something's not right about you," he said as he walked past her.

"Asia's always been a tomboy," Montana said.

"Whatever."

"Ladies, not here, please," Savannah stressed.

Troy made sure Savannah and her sisters got off the complex safely. Mike was sitting at a chair in his office when he returned.

"Don't even say it." Troy slid into his chair behind his desk.

"You must really love the oldest, huh?" Mike commented. "There's no way in hell, I would put up with that young one. What's her real name, anyway?" he asked.

"Mike, now you know I'm not at liberty to say."

"Her sister called her Asia."

"Foxy is her name," Troy insisted.

"Firefox would fit her better, because she's one piece of work."

"Looks like Mike has met his match."

"Now I know you don't want to go there, because you never did answer my original question."

Troy pretended not to know what he meant. His feelings for Savannah were under lock and key, and they would stay that way.

Troy and Mike both caught up on their pending projects. Before leaving, he instructed Cheryl on what to do in his absence. "I'll be working remotely. Mike will be in charge."

Mike assisted him with the boxes he needed. Each box contained special surveillance and tactical gear.

"I don't know what it is you're working on, but you know you don't have to do this alone, right?" Mike remarked.

"The less you know about this one, Mike, the better off it'll be for all of us."

"I got your back."

"I know that, man. Hit you up later."

He pulled out of the complex. He felt bad about not confiding in Mike. If need be, he would tell him everything. For now, though, he felt like he had everything under control.

Troy didn't know when the tail got ahold of him, because he was deep in thought about Savannah. Fortunately, he found out before he got near his neighborhood. He weaved in and out of traffic to make sure he wasn't being paranoid. Another look in his rearview mirror proved to him that he wasn't.

"So you want to play," he said out loud.

He decided to take whoever was following him through a maze and construction area. They were invading his personal time now, and he was long overdue for a nap. The person in the black car had no idea where they were. He could tell this from how they were driving. In fact, by the time they seemed to get control of the car, Troy was facing them head-on. The car swerved to avoid impact with Troy. They were welcomed with a few nails in the street and spun out of control. The car flipped on its side.

Troy stopped his SUV with his weapon drawn. This wasn't a heavily populated area, so he wasn't concerned about citizens witnessing this. However, someone could be looking over the rail from the highway above.

Before he could get to the car, the car burst into flames. He ran to the car to see if he could get the driver out, so he could beat him. The driver's neck appeared to be broken from the impact. Troy pulled out his phone and called an emergency response team.

He checked the wallet of the driver and made a mental note of who the driver was. He placed it back in the deceased's pocket and left the scene before the police arrived. He met a fire truck, which he assumed was going to the place of the accident.

Raymond was now sending men after him. He had every right to be concerned. His first two mistakes were crossing Major and scaring Major's girls. This was strike three, sending someone directly after him.

"I hope you're enjoying your freedom, Commander Steel, because come this time next year, you'll be either dead or locked up. I'll let you choose."

Troy sped home.

20

"Ladies, we don't have all day. I want to get there before noon!" Savannah shouted from the end of the stairway.

"Coming," Montana yelled back.

A few minutes later, Montana and Asia walked briskly down the stairway. "We know you're in a hurry to see your man, but you don't have to rush us," Asia stated as she grabbed an apple out of the bowl on the kitchen table.

"Whatever," Savannah snapped.

"Touchy. Somebody has a boyfriend," Asia teased.

"For the last time there's nothing going on between me and Troy."

"Heard it all before," Montana sang.

Savannah slammed the car door. Her sisters stood outside. "If you're not in by the time the garage door opens, you can walk."

They didn't test Savannah. They got in and didn't say much. They listened to a local morning show. After driving for a while Savannah turned the volume down on the stereo. "I owe you two an apology."

They both pretended like they didn't know what she was talking about. "We're cool," Asia said.

"I just have a lot on my mind, and you guys teasing me about Troy isn't helping any."

She turned the music back up to drown out her thoughts. Montana commented, "These are some nice houses."

Savannah pulled up to the gate and pressed zero. "It's us," she yelled. She smiled up at the camera.

The gate opened a few seconds later. "Nice," Asia said.

Troy met them at the doorway. "Glad you ladies could make it. Let me give you two the tour," Troy said.

Savannah lagged behind as Troy showed her sisters around. "Why don't you take them to your guest bedroom?" she teased.

"I would, but you wouldn't want your sisters to react the same way you did, now would you?" he responded.

"Of course not."

Montana waved her hand in between the both of them. "What's in the room you want us to see, Vanna?"

"Only a six-foot python," Savannah responded. The look on Montana's face was priceless. "Hey, you asked."

"Now, you know I hate snakes, girl."

"You and me both," Savannah said.

"Well, I don't. I want to see it," Asia said.

"You're sure?" Troy questioned. "It's feeding time, anyway. Want to watch?"

"Sure. Bye, ladies." Asia followed Troy to the guest room.

"I'm staying near the door, because if that thing gets out, I'm out," Montana said.

Savannah laughed. "You'll have to beat me to the door."

Savannah felt like she knew Troy's place, since this was her third time visiting. She led them into the study area. She and Montana went through the books on the shelf. "Did you know that you could kill a man by pinching his nerve in this area of the neck?" Montana asked as she used her hand to show the nerve she was speaking of.

"Troy showed me the move the other day."

Montana picked up book after book. Without looking at Savannah, she said, "I'm glad you talked me into doing the training. I've learned a lot these last few days."

"I know you think I'm a little controlling," Savannah said.

"A little."

"Okay, a lot. But I only do what I do to protect you two. You're all I have, and I don't plan on losing you."

"Girl, stop! You're going to make me cry."

They hugged each other. Asia and Troy returned to the room. "Aren't they cute? Bonding while we fed the snake." Asia faced Montana and outstretched her hands. "Girl, it was a big, long one too."

"Ugh," Montana responded.

"Troy, we're yours for the rest of the day. Tell us what we have to do," Savannah stated.

A wide grin spread across his face. "Don't pinch me, because I must be dreaming."

Montana said, "One Blake sister is all you could handle, and from the way things look, you're not even handling that one well, Mr. Troy." She folded her arms.

"My, my, my. Outsiders are not welcome," Troy teased.

Savannah said, "You best remember that."

"I love you, anyway, Savannah," he responded.

Savannah knew he was only using a figure of speech. She didn't want to imagine Troy still being in love with her after all this time. She pushed the "what-ifs" to the back of her mind. Troy led them to another room. He went directly to several boxes stacked in the corner of the room and placed them on a table.

"I feel like a kid at a candy store," Savannah said as she rushed toward the table and picked up a few items.

Troy responded, "It's playtime." He then picked up an item. "Savannah, you'll be my demonstrator.

"Asia, you'll be using this," he explained. "If you hook this up to the back of the computer, it'll track every keystroke, every Web page, every log-in, and every password on a computer." He passed the device to Asia.

She said, "It looks like an ordinary USB."

"Exactly. It's not meant to be noticed. It'll be your job to get these hooked up to various computers."

Savannah handed Troy another item. "This little thing has a camera in it. Watch this."

Troy pinned it on Savannah. Savannah could feel his hands shake a little. She looked in his eyes and flinched. What she saw staring her in the face frightened her. She looked away. "Savannah, go anywhere in the room."

Troy turned on a monitor. "Everywhere she goes, we see."

Montana said, "It's so pretty. I never would have thought to suspect a camera was part of it."

"You're not supposed to," Troy responded. "Here's one for each of you."

"Ooh, more goodies," Asia said.

"Savannah, hand me that box," Troy said.

"I know what this is. It's a wire," Savannah said while patting herself on the back.

"But not just any wire. This can't be detected. It's placed in a sensitive area, and unless someone puts a hand up your crack, he or she won't be able to detect it."

Montana said, "What? You don't have to worry about me using it."

Troy laughed. "Just kidding. One little piece of wire can record enough information to incriminate someone. What we normally do is insert in between the toes, or in the case of some women, they intertwine it with their hair. No one is any the wiser."

Savannah held the wire. "I'm impressed."

"Montana, you're going to like this." He opened up a box filled with hairpieces, makeup, and other accessories.

She stood up and went through the pieces. "You're trying to stay on my good side, aren't you?" she said.

Explaining the use of each one, Troy went through the rest of the items on the table. "I saved the best for last. These are items that can literally bring a man to his knees."

"Here I thought I was one of a kind," Savannah joked.

"That, dear, you are," Troy responded.

"Enough of the goo-goo eyes." Asia pretended to be annoyed.

Savannah rolled her eyes.

Troy said, "These are weapons. Weapons that, if used correctly, could be weapons of minor or mass destruction."

21

Troy enjoyed watching the excitement in Savannah's eyes. For a moment he got lost in her eyes. Her eyes were hypnotic, and he would bet she didn't even realize it. He explained what each weapon could do. He had triplicates of everything.

He held up a vial. "This could be fatal if you use too much, so you only need a drop to knock someone out."

Savannah reached for it. He was quicker. He put his hand behind his back. She said, "Let me try it on you."

"Uh, no." He pulled out a small brown bag containing what looked like grains of salt. "You can mix this in food. It'll work the same way as the other item. Use it sparingly." He looked at Savannah. "Remind me to use my test kit before I eat at your house again."

He continued to show them the other paraphernalia. Time stood still as he demonstrated item after item. It was late afternoon when he finished. "I hope you will join me for dinner tonight."

"I need to do some stuff for work," Asia said.

Montana added, "Me too. I took time off, but there are still some reports I need to look over at the house."

Troy answered, "You better go before it gets too late, then. Be careful and call us when you get home."

"Who said I was staying?" Savannah asked.

"You didn't say you were leaving also."

Asia and Montana grabbed their purses and their bags of goodies. "We're heading out now." Asia pointed to the door.

Montana added, "Seems like we're not wanted here, anyway."

"I'll walk you out," Troy said.

"They're my sisters, so I'll walk them out. What am I saying? I'm not staying," Savannah said.

"Please," he pleaded.

"Stay, we can find our way home," Montana said.

"Besides, we got a whole bag of arsenals. I doubt if anybody wants to mess with us." Asia had a "you don't want to bother me" look on her face.

"Fine. I know when I've been outnumbered." Savannah stormed out of the room.

"She'll be all right. Put some food in her stomach and you'll have her eating out of the palm of your hand," Montana said.

Troy walked them out and gave them directions on how to get back to the freeway.

"I'll bring her home before midnight."

"You better, because you don't want to get stuck with a frog," Asia joked.

Troy said, "I'll pretend like I didn't hear that."

He opened the gate and waited for them to exit before going to search for Savannah.

"Vanna. Savannah," he called out several times, but there was no response. He went from room to room. To his surprise he walked in on Savannah in the kitchen. He liked what he saw as she stood with one of his aprons on. Without looking his way, she continued to remove food from the refrigerator.

"Since I was coerced into staying, I thought I would help with the cooking," Savannah stated.

"A salad would go good with the steaks. I'll throw a couple on the grill," he said.

"Sounds like a plan."

Less than two hours later they were seated out on the patio, eating steak and a pasta salad Savannah had fixed.

"These homemade rolls are to die for," Troy said.

"I have to remember that for the next batch," Savannah said in between laughing.

"I've created a monster."

They worked together to clean up the kitchen. "Ouch," Savannah said as they bumped into each other.

Troy took Savannah in his arms and, without asking, kissed her. When she didn't pull away, he took it as a signal to tantalize her with his tongue.

She placed her hand around his neck and pulled him in closer. His hands roamed her body and he felt her body arch to his touch. The moan that escaped from her lips almost sent him over the edge. The member between his legs had a mind of its own. "Sa-van-nah, baby, if we don't stop, I won't be able to."

She gently touched his face. His body shivered at her touch. Her hand touching him was like a feather. It didn't tickle but sent a sensation through his body. "Did you mean what you said earlier?" Savannah asked.

Troy knew she was referring to his declaration of love earlier. The words were out of his mouth before he realized it, but now he couldn't bring himself to acknowledge his feelings. "When this is all over, we'll sit down and talk."

He couldn't tell if she was disappointed or not. If she was, she didn't press the issue. "I'll get my purse and things so you can take me home."

"Why don't you spend the night?" Troy asked. He didn't want her to leave. He wanted her in his arms.

Savannah said, "First you want me to stop; now you want me to stay. Make up your mind."

Troy felt like a fool. Apparently, he took too long to respond, because she left him in the kitchen, staring down at the member of his body that betrayed his true thoughts. He tried to think of something to calm himself down. It took a few moments for him to cool off.

Savannah's beautiful eyes stared back at him when he entered the living room. Troy wanted her to stay, but he didn't want her to be with him out of obligation. Some women looked at him as being a hero, when he was an average man looking for a woman who loved him for him. Truth was, up until reuniting with Savannah, he wasn't looking for a commitment. She made him want to settle down. That was scarier than his last assignment with The Agency.

"Earth to Troy," Savannah said as she stood next to him with her purse and bag filled with the items he showed her and her sisters earlier. He took the bag from her.

"Sorry about what happened in the kitchen," Troy said.

"Me too."

"I'll take you home now if you're ready."

They were soon on the road. Savannah didn't have much to say to Troy on the ride back to her place. He attempted to start conversations with her, but to no avail. During the silence Troy thought, *This is going to be a long ride.*

When they pulled up in front of her house, before she exited, Troy touched Savannah on the arm and said, "Wait."

"I've taken up enough of your time," Savannah responded.

"This thing between us." Troy hoped he didn't sound nervous.

"There's nothing between us. So whatever you were going to say, save it." Savannah left the car and slammed the door.

He watched her enter her house. He grabbed the bag she left behind and walked to her front door. He rang the doorbell. "You forgot your bag," he said, assuming Savannah would be on the other side of the opening door.

"I'll take it." Montana reached for the bag.

Disappointed, Troy responded, "Tell your sister, I'll see her in the morning."

Montana stood in the doorway, blocking Troy's view. She frowned. "I don't know what happened after we left, but I hope you're not playing emotional games with my sister."

Troy threw his hands up in defeat. "What happens between her and me is just that, between her and me."

Montana walked out of the house and closed the door. "If you care about her, and I mean really care about her, give her some time. Don't rush it."

Troy decided to confide in Montana. "Your sister doesn't trust me."

"Men are so stupid. If she didn't trust you, do you think she would have stayed behind? The thing is, she trusts you more than she has any other man . . . since Dad. All I can say is, if you don't plan on it being long-term, nip it now. Help us with this, and then stay out of her life."

Montana went back into the house, leaving him on the porch contemplating what she had just said. Troy had no intention of staying away from Savannah. He lost her once. He refused to lose her again. He would deal with this situation first, but as soon as they got some closure to Major's death, he and Savannah would talk and maybe even go on a real date. Hopefully, a date that wouldn't lead to disaster, since lately he seemed to have a knack for putting his foot in his mouth.

Troy pulled out Meeks's business card and dialed his number before pulling out of the driveway. "Can you meet me tonight?" he asked.

Meeks was already out and at a sports bar. Troy liked to avoid taverns, when he could, but he felt the bar was probably a better place than any to meet. Meeks found them a table away from the crowd. He and Meeks joked around a little before Troy decided to get down to business.

"Do you do any freelance work?" Troy asked.

"Every chance I get. Child support is killing me, man," Meeks responded.

"I need you to keep an eye out on someone. Well, actually a family."

"Sure. I usually work days, so as long as it doesn't interfere with my schedule, I can do it." Meeks's eyes wandered around the club.

"Great. I'll just need you to watch them from about one A.M. until it's time for you to go to your next shift."

"I can do that."

"Great." Troy slipped him an address. "Don't let them know you're watching them. These three women aren't your average women."

"Any of them fine?" Meeks asked.

"Real lookers," Troy responded.

Meeks smiled. "Don't worry. Whoever I'm protecting them from will have to go through me to get to them, and I'm not so easy to get rid of," Meeks said.

22

"Vanna, wake up," Montana said as she shook the bed.

"Go away," Savannah responded. She pulled the covers over her head and held it tight.

Montana sat on the bed. "We didn't say anything to you last night, but we know something happened between you and Troy. If he hurt you in any way, just say the word."

Savannah reluctantly pulled the covers down. "It's not him, it's me. I thought . . ." She threw the covers down. "Never mind. All's well."

"I'll say this, and then I'll go and let you get dressed. I think Troy cares about you. I think you care about him, but until you two are able to communicate this to one another, just chill. Find Dad's killer and then let things progress normally."

"When did you get so wise?"

"I learned from my older sister."

Savannah remained in bed a few more minutes. Her sisters had no idea of her history with Troy. She felt guilty keeping the information from them. How could she explain her feelings for Troy, when she didn't quite understand them herself? She dragged herself out of the bed and took a long shower. Feeling rejuvenated, Savannah met her sisters downstairs.

Less than an hour later, Montana pulled her SUV in front of Troy's house. He greeted them at the door. Troy spoke and acted like nothing had happened last night, so Savannah pretended the same. Minutes later they paired up and went separate ways. Savannah and Montana worked together on coming up with their new identities in one room, while Troy and Asia worked on gathering information about the men on the list provided by Major in another.

"We'll save Uncle Raymond for last," Savannah said.

"I want to be there to see it all." Savannah could hear the pain in Montana's voice. Out of all of the sisters, Montana was closest to Uncle Raymond.

Each pair reunited in the living room after they completed their tasks. Savannah's cell phone rang before Troy could talk. "It's my neighbor," she said, looking at the screen. She answered the call. "Are you sure it's the same men?" she asked. "No, don't do anything. Stay inside. I'll call the police." She hung up. The conversation around her ceased. "Ladies, we won't be going back home tonight. Seems like our visitors returned."

Montana removed her cell phone. "I'm calling the police—"

Troy interrupted their conversation. "Montana, don't. You need to go back home. If you don't, they may suspect something. This time if they come back, you'll be ready for them."

"My daddy once told me that an unwanted pest had to be terminated," Asia said as she folded her arms. "It's on."

Savannah's stomach turned cartwheels as they drove home. Troy stayed lying down on the floor, just in case they were being watched. "Troy, are you sure we're doing the right thing?" Savannah asked.

"Yes. We want them to come to you. If need be, we'll kill them all. Once I identify who the leader is, we can eliminate the others."

Savannah thought back to her conversation with her neighbor. "The short one is the one in charge."

"If the others don't want to cooperate, then we'll dispose of them."

Asia turned around in her seat. "Like you did with Ms. Irene."

"No, worse," Troy responded.

It took them an hour to set up for their visitors. Troy made sure the cameras on the outside would cover every angle. Each sister made sure she had her weapons near her. Savannah's nerves were on edge. Troy being there calmed her some. She hoped the men in black wouldn't return. Troy talked them into playing board games to combat their nervousness. When nightfall hit, they took turns sleeping in shifts. Nothing happened overnight.

Savannah cooked breakfast and watched them all eat. She didn't have an appetite, but she noticed Troy had no problem piling more and more food on his plate. Troy's phone rang, interrupting her thoughts.

"Ladies, I need to go into the office."

"I can drop you off," Montana volunteered.

"Savannah, I'll take the rest of this to go."

Savannah rolled her eyes, but she got up and placed his bacon and biscuits on a plastic plate and covered it with foil. Troy drank his juice and stood up from the table. Savannah followed behind them to the garage door.

Troy turned and said, "I know nothing happened last night, but still keep your guard up."

"I will," she responded.

"Promise me, you'll call me if you need me."

"I will."

Troy got in the front seat of Montana's SUV and then let the seat back so he couldn't be seen.

"I hate this," Asia yelled from behind Savannah. "Here we are playing the waiting game. I don't know if I want to live my life like this."

Savanna agreed. "It's time we turn it up a notch. Let's go pay Uncle Raymond a visit."

"But that's not in the plans," Asia said.

"No, it isn't. This is the plan." Savannah went over her idea of having Asia plant a device in their uncle Raymond's office. Thirty minutes later they were casually dressed and headed to The Agency's local office.

"Security there is like Fort Knox," Asia said as Savannah weaved through traffic.

"I know, but you're a computer engineer. You always carry junk with you, so they wouldn't suspect you of carrying anything in," Savannah said.

"True. Okay, I'm ready."

Asia rearranged her handbag and they exited the car. After going through numerous security checks, Savannah and Asia were escorted into the lobby of Commander Raymond Steel's office. The secretary knew they were Major's daughters. They took a few minutes to get caught up on each other's lives since Major's death.

"Uncle Raymond," they both sounded enthusiastic about seeing him. They each took turns hugging him.

"Girls, what are you doing here? Where's Montana?"

Savannah looped her arm through his. "She had to work. We just wanted to treat our favorite uncle to lunch."

"I don't know. I have so much stuff to do. See all of the stuff on my desk." He pointed to the stack of folders piled high on his oak desk.

"Well, I'm hungry. Come on."

"Unc, may I use your phone? I can never get a signal in here," Asia said, pretending to use her cell phone.

"Let me see it," he said.

"No. I would rather use a landline, anyway."

"Okay, we'll wait."

"No, go ahead. I'll meet you both downstairs," Asia insisted as she stood up to use the phone. Savannah watched her press the numbers. Savannah knew from their previous conversation, she was only calling her bank to check her balance.

She grabbed Uncle Raymond's arm. "She's a big girl. She knows how to find her way down."

"Don't keep us waiting too long. You got me hungry for a big old steak now," Raymond said while rubbing his stomach.

Savannah engaged him in conversation. She played on his ego and mentioned how proud her dad would be of him and all that he had done. She also reassured him that she was not going to deal with Troy. "I realized he's a man from my dad's past. I trust your judgment, and if you say he's bad news, then he's not a man I need to be hanging around."

"That's all I was saying, dear," Raymond said as he placed his arms around Savannah.

Savannah hoped Asia would hurry up. Raymond would be suspicious if it took her too long, and she didn't want that. They were about to get to the car, when she saw Asia running toward the door.

"There she is. You know how she can run her mouth," Savannah said.

"She gets that from your mama. Ellen Danielle could talk a grown man out of his paycheck," he joked. "That's how much she would talk."

Savannah faked a smile. How dare he talk about her mama? She wanted to slap the smug look off his face.

Asia sounded out of breath. "I hope I didn't keep y'all waiting too long."

"I was about to call my secretary to see where you were," he responded.

"The elevators took a while."

He glanced at his watch. "Where to girls? My treat."

"Since you're treating, let's do that new steak house right down the street from here," Savannah said.

Thirty minutes later, Savannah forced herself to eat with the enemy. Asia was a good actress. She laughed at the right time. They were only there for about an hour, but it seemed longer. Once they dropped him off and pulled out of the parking lot, Savannah released her breath as if she had been holding it the entire time.

"The recording device is in place, but now I just have to see how to go back and get it," Asia said.

"You won't. Montana will have to retrieve it."

"But she can't change a lightbulb, let alone remove a computer chip."

"We'll come up with something. You'll have to teach her. If we show up again, he'll be suspicious."

"Swing by my place so I can pick up some more clothes."

Savannah checked her rearview mirror to make sure they weren't being followed. When she entered Asia's apartment complex, she surveyed the area and didn't see any cars that looked out of place. She parked in an open space. "Be careful."

"I shouldn't be long," Asia said before closing the door.

Savannah waited behind in the car as Asia went to get her change of clothes. A black sedan passed through the parking lot. The windows were too tinted for her to see the occupants. Her instincts kicked in. She felt for her gun. Her heartbeat increased. *I'm just being paranoid, that's all it is,* she thought. She dialed Asia's number. Asia didn't pick up. She held on to her gun and slid from the driver's side.

~ *23* ~

Savannah filled Troy's waking thoughts. His quest to find Major's killer was first fueled by the loyalty he had for him, but now was fueled by the rekindled love he had for Major's daughter. Troy's call to Savannah went unanswered. He scrolled through his phone to locate Montana's number.

Montana sounded frantic. "Troy, I'm so glad it's you. Vanna and Asia aren't here, and I'm worried," she responded.

Troy turned away from the computer screen. "What do you mean they aren't there?"

"When I got back home, they were gone."

"I'm on my way there. If they come home before I get there, call me."

Troy grabbed his keys and jacket. "Cheryl, call me on my cell if you need me," he said as he rushed out of the office. The elevator seemed to take too long, so Troy opted to take the stairs. He rushed past his employees and sped out of the parking lot. His gut instincts alerted him that Savannah could be in trouble.

Troy broke all traffic laws and made it to the Blake sisters' house in record time. Montana opened the door before he could ring the doorbell. "They're not answering the phone," she said.

"Right now, all we can do is wait," Troy said as he followed Montana to the living room.

Montana paced back and forth. "This is unlike Asia. She sleeps with the phone up to her ear."

Troy tried to concentrate. He needed Montana calm. "What grocery store does Savannah normally go to? It's possible they went shopping, and sometimes cell phones don't work in certain parts of stores."

Montana said, "Brookshire's, but the fridge is full, so . . ."

His phone vibrated in his pocket. When Savannah's name displayed across the screen, he let out a breath he must have been holding. He was not prepared for her frantic voice on the other end.

"Calm down. I can't understand you. Speak slowly," Troy soothed.

"Asia's hurt. I didn't know who else to call."

"Where are you?"

"We're at Asia's apartment."

"We're on our way." He grabbed Montana's arm. "Come on. I need you to show me how to get to Asia's place."

Montana barely had enough time to grab her keys before Troy dragged her out of the house. She locked the door and jumped in the passenger side of his SUV.

"I don't want you to panic, but Asia's hurt."

"What?" Montana pulled out her cell phone.

Troy reached over and grabbed it. "You can't use that anymore." He let the window down and threw it out the window.

Montana commenced cursing him out. "I can't believe you trashed my phone."

"Did you not hear anything I said the other day? There's GPS tracking on those phones, and if anybody is looking for you or tracking your moves, guess what, all they have to do is track your cell phone."

She hung her head. "I need to use your phone."

Troy gave her his phone.

"Vanna, how's Asia?"

Troy couldn't hear Savannah's response. "What exit?" he asked Montana.

"It's the second one on the left," she replied. "We're a few minutes away," she informed Savannah, and hung up. "It's the next apartment complex," Montana informed Troy. He spotted Savannah's car.

"Which apartment?" he asked as he pulled up behind Savannah's car. He didn't care about blocking anyone in.

Montana jumped out of the vehicle and he followed her up the stairs. She knocked and he waited.

"Thank God," Savannah said, hugging Montana.

She looked in Troy's direction. She looked relieved to see him. Propped on the couch was Asia. Out of habit Troy did a quick survey of her spacious apartment. Asia's fixation with exotic things was apparent with the paintings and artifacts displayed throughout.

Troy said, "What happened?"

Asia rubbed the back of her head. She eased up on the sofa. Savannah propped a pillow behind her. "I came up to get some clothes. My front door was closed, but it was unlocked. I couldn't remember if in my haste to get to Vanna's, I had locked it or not. I was only in the apartment a few minutes, when out of nowhere, I felt a thump on the back of my head. The next thing I remember is hearing Vanna wailing."

Savannah stepped in. "Shh . . . I'll tell him the rest." She turned her attention toward Troy. "I was downstairs waiting and waiting. Too much time had passed, I thought, so I phoned to hurry her up. When I didn't get a response, I got my gun and came on up."

"Was the door open when you got here?" Troy asked.

"No, but it was unlocked," Savannah responded.

"Did you see anything suspicious?"

"Yes. I saw this black sedan in the parking lot. I thought it was strange. It wasn't like they were looking for a parking spot, because there were plenty of those."

"You didn't see anyone come down or on your way up to Asia's apartment?"

"No. Believe me, I've been replaying those minutes back and forth, and I don't recall seeing anyone or anything."

Troy said, "Whoever did this found an alternate exit."

"The balcony," Asia answered. She pointed toward the balcony.

Troy stood up and walked to the glass door. It was closed but unlocked. "That's how they got in and got out." He jiggled the latch. "This was an easy entry. Not a secure lock at all."

"Wow, thanks," Asia managed to say.

Troy looked at Montana. "Call a locksmith."

Troy walked out onto the balcony. Some of Asia's plants had been knocked over. He bent down to examine a footprint. From the size of the footprint in the dirt, Troy made the intruder out to be male. He picked up the turned-over flowerpots and sat them upright. He surveyed around the balcony to see if the intruder had left any evidence. He looked over the balcony to see how the intruder had escaped. It wouldn't have taken much to climb up to the second floor and get out. A simple rope would have done the trick. The person Savannah saw driving around the parking lot was probably the lookout guy. Something brown caught Troy's eye. He reached his hand in between the leaves of the plant and pulled out a brown wallet. "Lucky me," he said.

He held the wallet up and reviewed the ID. The name matched the name on the list from Major's file. Troy placed the wallet in his pocket. For now, he would keep his discovery to himself. He examined the rest of Asia's apartment. He could tell she was a techie from all of the computer and computer accessories in almost every room.

"All is secure," he said as he took a seat at the dining-room table that sat directly toward the living room.

"Troy, thanks for being there for us," Savannah said as she got up.

"No thanks needed."

Montana went with Asia to her bedroom so she could pack up some more stuff.

"I guess she spooked whoever it was that came here, so they didn't get a chance to get anything," Troy said.

Savannah responded, "I'm just glad that's all it was. My heart skipped a few beats when I rushed into her apartment and saw her lying there."

Before Troy could respond, someone knocked on the door. He drew out his weapon. "I got it."

He looked out the peephole and put his gun back in his pocket. "It's the locksmith," he said to Savannah before he opened the door.

"Come on in," Troy said.

"A lady called. Said you guys needed a new lock," the round-faced brown-haired man said.

"Follow me," Troy responded.

Troy informed the locksmith of what type of lock he wanted installed. "You sure you haven't done this before," the man joked.

"Positive," Troy responded.

An hour later, Troy was satisfied that the windows and all of the doors were now secure. He paid the locksmith and gave him a generous tip.

"If you need anything else, don't hesitate to call me," the locksmith stated before he left.

Asia hugged Troy. "Thanks for everything."

Troy hugged Asia back. She reminded him of the sister he had lost. He didn't have time to mourn. He snapped out of it. "Ladies, let's get moving. You all can stay at my place tonight."

"I need some clothes," Montana said.

"Me too," Savannah added.

They went in two separate cars, but they followed each other to Montana's town house and then back to Savannah's to retrieve their things. Troy knew the time to implement their plan was at hand. It was time to set their plan in motion.

~ 24 ~

Troy gave up his room to Savannah. She tossed and turned the first few hours of trying to sleep, so she decided to go downstairs to get something to drink. Maybe if she could warm up some milk, it would help her rest. She didn't expect to see Troy, with a pair of pajama bottoms and a bare chest, looking sexy, doing the same thing.

"I couldn't sleep either," Troy stated, as if he read her mind. "Here, I made enough for two."

He poured her a cup. She sat on the bar stool at the counter and sipped it. "That hits the spot," she said as she closed her eyes and leaned her head back, enjoying the taste.

Troy joined her by sitting on the bar stool next to her. "It's the cinnamon. It adds the zing to it."

She opened her eyes and looked at him. "I like it."

"Savannah, we need to talk. We can't go on with this tension between us," Troy said.

"I thought we squashed that. I mean, you're my hero. You were there when I needed you." Savannah stared into the cup of milk.

He reached over and placed his hand over her other hand. "I'll always be there for you."

The palms of her hands sweated. She hoped he couldn't feel her increased pulse. "Thanks." She brought the cup up to her lips and used it as a time to remove her other hand from under his. She drank the rest of the milk. "I think I'll sleep better now." She got up from the stool. "Thanks again."

Troy didn't say anything. Savannah was getting under the covers, when she heard a slight knock at her door. "Come in," she responded.

She was expecting to see one of her sisters. Instead, Troy stood there, looking like the man of her fantasies. The moonlight beaming through the curtains hit his chest, making the hair on his chest seem to shine a darker black. No words passed between them. Troy seemed to glide toward the bed. Without saying a word he got in the bed and embraced her. She was asleep seconds later. She didn't have any nightmares; in fact, she couldn't recall dreaming at all.

When she woke up the next morning, she was in bed alone. A part of her felt that the vision of Troy coming to her room must have been a dream, but he left a reminder. A red rose, with a note under it on the pillow next to her.

She smelled the rose before reading the note: *I didn't want to disturb you, so I let you sleep. Thank you for last night. I needed it more than you realized.*

She folded the note and placed it on the table beside the bed, along with the rose. She went to the bathroom and showered and dressed before going to check on her sisters. She followed the laughter. They were downstairs talking to Troy.

"There she is." Asia got up and hugged her.

"Glad to see you're doing better," Savannah noted.

"We were going over our game plan for today," Montana said.

"And you didn't wait for me." Savannah pretended to be insulted. "I see you all have bonded in my absence."

"Eat up, because today is your first mission," Troy said. He placed a plate filled with food in front of her.

Savannah's stomach was relieved. She hadn't eaten anything since lunchtime the day before. After breakfast they met up in Troy's home office.

"I found out that one of the guys on the list has a standing monthly appointment with a psychiatrist. You'll be subbing for his regular psychiatrist."

"How will we pull that off? What about the real doctor and the secretary?"

"Already got you covered. Montana has volunteered to be the bait. She's going to be so psychotic that the secretary and the doctor will be occupied for a while in another office. That'll give you and Asia enough time to talk to suspect number one."

"What if it doesn't work?" Savannah asked.

"Trust me, it'll work," Troy said. "Besides, if all else fails, I'll pretend to be a robber and hold them hostage until I feel you're through."

"For some reason that doesn't make me feel any better," Savannah responded.

"No time to second-guess. Time is of the essence," he stated.

Montana said, "Come on. I need to work on your and Asia's appearance."

Troy went over key points about Redford with Savannah. She made her notes. Troy tested the hidden recording device to make sure it was positioned correctly on her shirt. They waited in the parking lot for Montana to use her device to signal them it was okay to make their way into the office.

"We only have a fifteen-minute window, so, Asia, I'm counting on you to be Savannah's backup," Troy said as they exited the car.

Savannah and Asia slipped past the security guard and went to the seventh floor.

"Make sure it's Redford before you send him in the office," Savannah said to Asia.

"I know what I'm doing," Asia responded.

"We'll see."

"Where's the confidence?" Asia smiled. Savannah went into the doctor's office. Redford's file was already out on the desk. She quickly thumbed through it.

"Your four o'clock is here," Asia's voice came over the intercom.

"Send him in," Savannah responded.

Redford, a brawny-looking man, seemed startled when Savannah turned the chair around. "Where's Dr. Monroe?" he asked.

"She had an emergency, but wanted me to step in because she didn't want you to have to reschedule."

He backtracked. "I'll come back later."

Savannah used her feminine wiles. She stood up. She removed the hairpins holding her hair together and loosened her hair. He watched as the curls fell to her shoulders. "From what she briefed me on, you really can't afford to miss an appointment."

"I guess I can stay," he said as he sat down on the couch.

She picked up his folder and a recorder. She sat in the chair next to the couch and crossed her legs. She made sure to show more skin than what she would normally show. "I know it might be difficult to talk to a new doctor, but I assure you, you are in good hands."

He stuttered, "I don't kn-know. Dr. Monroe, she knows all there is to know about me."

"Pretend I'm her," she responded.

He giggled. "I wish. You're far more attractive than she is."

"Thank you for the compliment, but it isn't about me. It's all about you." She reached out and touched his hand.

She listened to him talk about some of his emotions. Her ears didn't perk up until he mentioned his current assignment. "Doc, I want to get out of this, but I'm in too deep. My boss is a pig. He has me . . ." He paused. "What I say here is confidential, right?" he asked.

"Yes. Nothing goes past these four walls," she assured him.

"Well, he's stabbed his own friend in the back, so why should I trust him? I want to get out, but I'm in too deep."

Savannah contemplated her approach. "You're only accountable for your own actions, not others." She continued, "Coming here and talking it out can help. What is it that you don't want to do?"

"He wants me to cause problems for one of my ex-colleagues. I can't. The man he's sending me after is a good man. He was one of the best we had, until he got out. Lucky him."

Savannah read in between the lines. She knew "cause problems" was the equivalent to kill. She twitched as she thought about the threat on Troy's life. "You can always say no," Savannah suggested.

"I have no choice. The way they are trying to cause him problems, they can turn on me. I have two kids. I can't let that happen."

"What if there was a way out? What if there was another solution?" Savannah suggested. "Would you take it?"

"In a heartbeat," he responded.

"Seriously, I might have a solution to your problem." Savannah hoped Troy heard everything and would take the initiative to come help her out.

"If you could help me, Doc, I would gladly take you up on your offer."

"I need my assistant for a moment."

Savannah made the mistake of turning her back on Redford. He had his arms around her neck before she could get to the door.

"You think you're smart, don't you? Your voice sounded so familiar. I just remembered where I heard it. What did you do to Dr. Monroe?"

Savannah remembered the move Troy had taught her. Redford loosened his grip and fell back when she used the heel of her shoe and dug into his leg.

"You, bi . . ." Before he could get it out, Troy burst through the door with Asia behind him. Troy punched him a few times.

"Are you okay?" Troy asked Savannah.

Asia asked, "Why didn't you press the alert button?"

"I was in the process of doing that, when the jerk grabbed me." Savannah rubbed her neck.

"Okay, we need to get him out of here, before the real doctor returns. Asia, help Savannah straighten up while I think of a way to get him out of here."

Asia and Savannah made sure the room looked like it appeared before the incident. They used some wipes Troy had given them to remove their fingerprints. Savannah pinned her hair back up.

"You're going to pretend you guys are a couple," Troy said. "Let him lean on you. He's awake enough to walk on his own, though."

Redford was disoriented but did as instructed. Savannah pretended he was hugging her, just in case the camera was activated before they could get out of its view.

Asia took the elevator down. Savannah, Redford, and Troy took the stairs. "Okay, I got him," Troy said as he flipped him over his shoulder.

Savannah ran down the stairs as fast as she could. Asia had the car pulled up as close as she could to where the stairway ended in the parking garage. Troy looked around and placed him in the backseat. "I'll sit back here with him, just in case he fully awakes. Asia, switch seats with Savannah, and I need you to reactivate the security cameras."

They did as instructed. Once Asia gave the okay that her task was completed, Savannah drove out of the garage as if nothing had happened.

"That's Montana," Asia said as she clicked the phone on speaker.

"I need one of you to come check me out," she said. "I'm in the psych ward. They will only release me to a relative."

"See, I always told you, you were crazy. Now you're certified," Asia joked.

"You better be glad I'm here."

"Talk nice," Savannah said as they rolled down the highway.

Troy jumped in the conversation. "I'll send a buddy of mine to get you. Meet us back at my house."

"Who? How will I know I can trust him?" Montana asked.

"You won't know, but you can trust me," Troy responded.

"Look, Montana, you're not in a position to be making any demands. Do as the man says. Chill. Someone will be there to get you," Savannah said before she disconnected the call.

"Meeks, I need a favor. I need you to check someone out of the psych ward," Troy said to his friend. "She's under the name Constance. April Constance. Pretend like you're Mr. Constance. It'll work out fine."

"Don't worry, I'll take care of it," Meeks responded from the other end of the phone.

Their passenger stirred. Troy ended his conversation abruptly. "Look, I have to go. If you run into any trouble, hit me on my cell." He disconnected the call with Meeks. "Your sister will be in good hands."

He heard Savannah let out a sigh. Redford attempted to sit up, but couldn't because he was tied up. He opened up his eyes and stared into Troy's cold black eyes. Troy said, "Redford, you picked the wrong man to come after."

"Man, I had no choice."

"You always have choices."

Troy could see the fear in Redford's eyes. Redford's sinister laugh was a failed attempt to mask his fear.

"I'll do anything. Just let me go. My kids. My two sons will miss me." Redford was begging for his life.

"Shut up. If I was going to kill you, I would have done it an hour ago."

"What do you want?"

"You ask too many questions," Troy responded.

Savannah pulled up to the gate. He handed her a card. He assisted their extra passenger into his house. "You ladies don't have to wait. I got this."

Savannah crossed her arms. "No, I'm not going any-where."

Troy didn't argue with Savannah. "Let's move this party down to the dungeon."

"Dungeon. Man, I don't like closed-up areas," Redford complained.

Troy laughed. "I know. That's why we're going."

Redford protested, but Troy dragged him down, any-way. "Asia, wait at the door. I need for you to listen for the doorbell. It's hard to hear down here."

Asia said, "Man, I miss all of the fun."

Redford looked at them all. "You people are sick."

"Not as sick as you're going to be if you don't tell me what I want to know," Troy said as he pushed in a chair.

Troy pulled up another chair, turned it around, and then sat down. "So who is trying to get rid of me, and why?"

"You know I can't tell you that."

Troy looked at Savannah. "Turn the lights down a little. It's too much light."

Savannah went to the light switch and turned the knob.

"No, don't!" Redford yelled.

"Don't tell me a big old burly man like you is scared of the dark," Savannah heckled.

Troy added, "It's funny how an assassin can have fears, just like the rest of us."

"You're as good as dead, and you"—Redford looked in Savannah's direction—"You're going down with him."

Savannah walked and stood in front of him. "I should have used my other heel and messed up your other leg."

Troy had created a dangerous interrogator. "We don't have all day."

"The commander said you were a threat to our operation. I was only following directions."

"Did those directions include killing me?" Troy asked.

"If it took that." Redford looked him in the eyes and didn't flinch.

Troy was tired of playing around. He stood up and flipped over the chair that Redford was sitting in. Redford fell to the floor. "Time is running out," Troy stated.

"You know too much. Commander feels like Major collaborated with you."

Before Troy could respond, Savannah stepped in. "Did you kill my father?"

"No, that's one assignment I refused to take."

In a quiet voice she asked, "Then who did?"

"I'm not at liberty to say," he responded.

Before Troy could react, Savannah stood by where Redford now sat on the floor and kicked him. Redford knew not to attempt to retaliate because at this point Troy didn't need a reason to take him out. Troy let Savannah release her frustrations before intervening.

"They're here," Asia called downstairs.

"Press the button I showed you before!" Troy shouted back. "Back to you."

"Commander said Major was going to expose us. All of us. You dropping out of The Agency made us think you had no loyalty to us anymore. We—"

Troy was livid and interrupted Redford. "I dedicated ten years to The Agency. My loyalty stopped the day Major was killed. You might not have pulled the trigger, but you were on the team that did. For that, you, too, will pay." Troy pulled out his gun and pointed it at Redford's forehead. Savannah's hands went up to her mouth in surprise. "You might want to leave us alone for a bit," Troy suggested.

"Don't. He's not worth it. Take him where you took the other one. He's not worth it." Savannah walked over and touched Troy on the shoulder.

He put the gun down. "She saved your life. I was a trigger away from sending you to hell." Troy placed the gun on the table. He reached down and pulled Redford up from the floor. "Sit down."

Redford was sweating by now. He said, "Even if you get rid of me, he's only going to keep sending someone else."

Troy asked, "What does he think happened to Irene?"

"He figured she went underground. What do you know about Irene?"

"The Terminator has been terminated," Troy stated.

Redford hung his head down. "She was a good agent."

"'Good' and 'Irene' shouldn't be in the same sentence," Troy stated.

Savannah asked, "Do you think it's wise for me to leave you two alone? I need to go check on Montana."

Troy looked at Redford. "It all depends on him. If he has one more smart comment to make, he's history."

Savannah looked at Redford. "I saved you once. Next time you might not be so lucky."

He watched her as she ascended the stairs. "She's a looker," Redford commented.

Troy laughed. "You're seconds away from being blown away and you're focusing on a woman looks. Pathetic. No wonder most women think we're dogs."

"You have the hots for her the way you're acting. Man, if the commander knew that, he would flip," Redford commented.

"You won't be talking to the commander anytime soon," Troy responded. "Answer this last question and then we can proceed."

"Why torture the girls? You know that's what he calls them." Redford laughed. "Never trust a man who will cause harm to his own family. Or in this case adopted family."

"Get to the point."

"He found out one of them was poking into things they shouldn't have been. We were sent to shake them up a bit. No real harm was going to come to them. Major had some information with our names on it. Once we found that, life as they knew it would have gone back to status quo."

"Tell me this. How could life go back to normal for them? One of you flunkies killed Major."

"That's where you're all wrong. Major was killed . . ." Redford didn't finish his statement. His body went into an uncontrollable spasm.

Troy realized at that moment he was having a seizure. He didn't have anything to keep his tongue from choking him. He knew enough not to use his hand, because the person in the seizure could lock onto it, and it wouldn't be good for either one of them. Redford died right there in front of Troy.

He didn't know how he was going to break it to the Blakes, but it may have been for the best. Redford would not have survived in the exile he called The Dungeon. Not with his phobia. He knew enough about him to know he would rather have committed suicide than be locked up like a dog.

He needed to get Meeks out of the house. He didn't need to know that Redford had expired. Meeks was sworn to uphold the law, and he didn't want to put Meeks in a compromising position.

~ 26 ~

Savannah was shocked to see Dion Meeks sitting and chatting with Montana when she arrived upstairs. He was Montana's ex, and if memory served her correctly, they didn't end on such good terms. Montana caught him cheating, and he ended up marrying the woman after she got pregnant.

She listened as he updated them on what he had been doing since high school. "This is really a small world," Asia said.

Savannah added, "Six degrees of separation."

Montana looked to be fine. She said, "Imagine how I felt when he showed up to check me out."

"The expression on your face when you saw me was priceless."

"If I would have done what I was thinking, I would still be there, trust me," she responded.

Asia asked, "So why did you divorce?"

"It's complicated. Let's just say, things didn't work out."

Montana looked at Asia and answered, "I heard she cheated. Karma is something else." Savannah kicked Montana's leg under the table. "I'm just saying."

Savannah motioned for Troy to sit by her. "Your friend and my sister used to date."

From the look on his face, Troy was surprised. "Small world."

"That's what I said," Asia chimed in.

"Meeks, thanks, man."

"Anytime. Man, your place is huge. Business must be good," Meeks commented.

"Let me show you around. I wanted to talk to you about something, anyway," Troy said while getting up.

Savannah scooted over closer to Montana. "Girl, I know you wanted to croak when you saw him."

"So many memories came back to mind," Montana said. She started talking about a few good memories, and then the last memory of finding out he cheated.

Asia said, "He's looking good."

"You're so shallow," Montana retorted.

"So tell us about the ride over," Savannah said.

"Do you know he had the nerve to say he wouldn't have cheated if our dad didn't intervene and tell him he didn't want him dating me?"

"I can believe that," Savannah said.

Asia said, "I would have left you alone, too, if I had to deal with Dad."

"That's the thing. He just should have broken up with me. He didn't have to cheat." Sadness swept across Montana's face.

"Maybe, but that's water under the bridge now," Savannah said. "Let us tell you about our guest downstairs."

Savannah updated Montana on what had happened. Asia didn't say anything in front of Meeks because of the pact the sisters had made about trusting folks. Montana was amazed at what Savannah was telling her.

"I still can't believe Uncle Raymond would go to this extreme," Montana said.

"He has, and I'm just glad Dad isn't here to witness this betrayal," Asia stated.

"Ladies, I think Uncle Raymond may be the trig-german," Savannah confessed. "Think about it. When I arrived at the house, it didn't look to be disturbed. Whoever killed Dad had to be someone he knew, because he would have gone out with a fight, otherwise. The person had to have caught him off guard."

Montana and Asia thought about it. Asia spoke first. "You're right. I remember you telling us how the door was locked and nothing seemed to be out of place."

"In order to bring Uncle Raymond down, we're going have to get a confession from someone on that list. We have two down, and two more to go," Savannah said.

Montana said, "I'm over Dion. But him being here is making me uncomfortable."

"Just ignore him," Asia stated.

"If he wasn't so doggone sexy, I could," Montana said.

Asia's mouth dropped open.

Montana continued, "There I said it."

They shared a private laugh just as Troy and Dion returned to the room.

Dion said, "Ladies, it was a pleasure seeing you all again, especially you, Montana, but I have to go."

Savannah looked at Montana. "Walk him to the door."

If looks could kill, Savannah would be dead. Montana mumbled some things that Savannah couldn't hear.

Troy remained standing. "Ladies, we have a situation."

Savannah held her head down in disgust. "What now?"

Troy informed them of their guest's unexpected demise.

Asia stood up. "How are we going to get rid of a body without the police finding out?" She held her hand up to her mouth. "The police *was* just here. What if Dion got wind of this? This place will be swarming with police."

"Calm down," Troy said. "We don't want him to hear you now, do we?"

Savannah walked to where Asia stood and put her arms around her to calm her down. "We have to trust Troy to handle this." Savannah looked at Troy. "And we do trust you to take care of this."

Troy's eyes said what his mouth didn't. Savannah felt relieved. Troy left her and Asia in the room huddled up.

When Montana returned to the room, Savannah gave her an update. Montana said, "I don't know about you all, but this has been one hectic day. Are we staying here or going home?"

All eyes were on Savannah. Savannah made a decision for all three of them to return to their family home. "If we're going home, we need to leave now before it gets dark."

"We can leave some of our stuff here, just in case we have to come back," Montana suggested.

"True. Well, y'all go get your stuff together and I'll meet y'all at the front in about fifteen minutes," Savannah said.

Savannah went to look for Troy. She figured he would be in the dungeon, so that was the first stop she made. "Troy, we're going home tonight," she said.

"I don't think it's safe," Troy stated without hesitation.

"We'll be fine. You're only a phone call away, right?" Savannah knew that now wasn't the time for joking, but she wanted to ease the situation.

Troy stopped what he was doing. He removed the black gloves he was wearing and walked up to Savannah. "Promise me, you'll call. Even if you hear a cat screeching," Troy said.

"Promise." Savannah was sure Troy could hear her swallow. He was so close that Savannah could feel Troy's breath.

Savannah turned to walk up the stairs. Troy turned her around. Without waiting for an acknowledgment, Troy planted his lips on top of hers. Time stood still as they explored the depths of each other's mouths.

Troy released her after a long embrace. He held her hand and led her up the stairs. He playfully patted her on her behind before they were in the sight of her sisters. She popped him on the arm. The sound was loud enough for her sisters to hear, because they turned around.

"I'm ready," Savannah said while she gave Troy the evil eye.

Troy hugged Montana and Asia. "Call me when y'all make it home," Troy said to Savannah.

"I'll think about it," Savannah responded.

"You're so stubborn," Troy commented.

"And that's what you love about me," Savannah responded as she blew a kiss at him, then followed behind her sisters.

Savannah waved at him as she entered the passenger seat of Montana's vehicle.

"Between you and Montana, y'all make me sick," Asia said from the backseat.

"Girl, please. Troy is just a means to an end."

"End of your singlehood," Asia joked.

"That'll be the day," Savannah responded. She knew she was fighting a losing battle.

Troy removed all traces of Redford from his house. He made sure whoever found him would not be able to trace it back to him. If Redford hadn't had any kids, Troy would have made his body disappear for good. He hated he died, but it may have been best. He would keep what he knew about Redford's involvement sealed for his kids' sake.

Savannah left Troy a message to inform him that they had arrived safely. Keeping Redford's declaration in mind, he wasn't too keen on Savannah being out of his sight. She was equipped to handle herself, but it didn't make it easier.

In the meantime he had a business to run. He was long overdue for an update on some of the projects his staff was handling. He called Cheryl and had her update him. It was way past midnight by the time Troy got off the last call. Satisfied that all was well, Troy went to bed.

Troy never used alarms to wake him up. His body had an automatic time clock. He woke up to the sound of the phone ringing. He sat straight up when Savannah's distressed voice came from the other end. "She's gone" was all he could make out.

"Vanna, if you don't calm down, I can't hear you." He jumped out of bed and put on his clothes as Savannah tried to explain to him what had happened.

"Montana, she's gone. She left a note that she was going to go meet Uncle Raymond, and she's not answering her phone."

Troy was heading out the door before Savannah could finish telling him what had happened. "Where's Asia?"

"Right here. She's going out of her mind," Savannah responded.

"If she met him at the office, sometimes the phones don't work up there," Troy said, hoping he was correct.

"Something just isn't right," Savannah said. "She is so pigheaded. I told her not to trust Uncle Raymond."

Troy knew now wasn't the time to remind Savannah that being pigheaded must be a family trait, because Savannah, likewise, was not the easiest person to get along with at times. He sped down the highway.

"I'll be there soon. Call me if she returns, or if you hear from her before I get there," he said, then disconnected the call.

Troy dialed Meeks's phone number. He left a message for him to return his call. Meeks called him back a few minutes later. Meeks sounded out of breath. "Did I catch you at a bad time?" Troy asked.

"No, just working out," Meeks responded.

"What I'm about to tell you has to stay between us," Troy stated.

"Sure, man. You know you can trust me."

Troy asked him to meet him at the Blakes'.

They pulled up in the driveway at nearly the same time.

"Thanks, man, for coming. I need your help in locating Montana," Troy said as they walked toward the front door.

"Montana. What do you mean help finding her?" Meeks said in a low voice.

Before Troy could elaborate, Savannah had opened the front door. She rushed into his arms. Troy hugged her tight. "Come on. Let's take this inside," Troy said.

"Dion, thanks for coming," Asia said. Her eyes were red and puffy.

They all sat in the living room. Savannah snuggled up next to Troy as he tried to soothe her. Asia held on to the phone as if it were her lifeline.

"Savannah, I need you to calm down and tell Dion what you told me," Troy stated.

Savannah repeated everything. Troy rubbed the outside of her hand for comfort. "I need to look around," Troy said.

"Where's her room?" Dion asked.

"Dion, Montana doesn't live here," Asia responded.

"Oh, I thought you all lived together."

"No, we're just staying here for now," Asia said.

"While you two talk, Savannah, please show me the note."

Savannah led him to the kitchen. She handed Troy the message. He viewed it several times. "Her handwriting doesn't seem like it was written in distress."

"You can tell that from reading her note?" Savannah had a confused look on her face.

"Another one of my skills," Troy said. "Where's Asia's laptop?"

"Follow me." She led him to Asia's old bedroom.

Troy logged on. "I see she has the icon of the golden eagle."

Savannah stated, "I told you Dad equipped us well on some things."

"I see. If he trusted her to access the golden eagle's database, I know he must have felt this day would be coming."

Troy reviewed phone records. "This is strange. He didn't mention he talked to Montana."

Savannah leaned over his shoulder to see what he was talking about. "Only number I recognize is Uncle Raymond's."

Troy wasn't sure if he should tell Savannah or not. For the moment he would keep the identity of the phone number to himself.

"Savannah, we'll get Montana back okay. I need to do some further investigating. I'll pay Raymond a visit."

"But that'll blow our cover. He'll know that we're working together." Savannah was upset. "I don't know what to do."

"If he has Montana under lock and key, then he already knows," Troy reminded her.

Savannah's hands shook. "Do what you feel is best. I just need to find my sister."

Troy and Dion left at the same time. While they walked to the car, Troy asked, "Did Montana call you?"

"Yes. We talked briefly. She said she was heading out. We were supposed to meet for lunch," Dion stated.

Troy was satisfied with his answer. "Man, we can use all of your help. Off the record, though, because if she was taken by who I think she was taken by, we don't need the cops involved."

"I'll do whatever I can to help." Dion's cell phone vibrated. He looked at the caller ID. "That's the job. I'm on this. I won't let her go that easily this time around. So whoever has her will have to deal with me."

Troy responded, "Thanks, man. Just call me or Savannah if you come across anything that might help."

Troy waited for Dion to leave. He sat in his vehicle a few more minutes before leaving to go to The Agency.

Troy could tell from the expression on some of the faces that they were just as surprised to see him as he was to see them. When he left The Agency, he had no plans on ever returning to the building. Nothing much had changed. Folks were still running around to their destinations without any concern for what else was going on around them. One thing about The Agency, they were known to be able to program or deprogram many men and women, but a few like him, and like Major, could be tamed but never trained to think in what they termed "one mind."

What surprised Troy was the fact that he still had clearance to come and to go on the site as he pleased. Apparently, someone higher up, mainly his ex-commander, didn't think to remove him from the list. Now here he was on an elevator up to visit his ex-boss. He hoped Montana would be sitting in there in a long, drawn-out conversation. He hoped her disappearance was only a small misunderstanding.

Before heading to Raymond's office, he made a detour. After shooting the breeze with one of his ex-comrades, the former coworker bragged about how he put together the security system that The Agency now used. His ex-comrade was proud to show him some stuff. Troy played on that emotion. "Prove that your updates enhanced my system. Show me everybody who came in and out this morning."

"Sure," the ex-colleague replied.

"Man, I know you're not supposed to, but can I have a copy of that?" Troy asked.

It only took the man a few minutes to copy it. He handed the disc to Troy. "Well, from what I see so far, you did a great job," Troy said. "If I need any pointers, I'll definitely be calling you."

"Anytime, but it'll cost you," his ex-comrade joked.

Troy left that floor and headed to his original destination. No one was at the receptionist desk, so he entered

Raymond's office without knocking. Raymond swiveled his chair around at the sound of the door opening. He looked like he had seen a ghost. He reached for his drawer.

"No need. This is a friendly visit. Well, unless you decide not to make it so," Troy said as he walked to the desk and plopped down in the black leather chair opposite Raymond.

"Have to hand it to you. You got some balls," Raymond said as he leaned back in his chair.

"I learned from the best." Troy picked up a cigar out of the box on Raymond's desk. He smelled the cigar and placed it in his pocket. "This will be good later."

"What do you want?" Raymond said without cracking a smile.

"First I wanted to let you know that you need to hire new recruits. The ones you sent after me aren't up to par."

"I don't know what you're talking about."

"Sure, but maybe you do know what happened to Montana." Troy sat straight up in his chair and tried to see if Raymond's gestures would signal that he knew more than what he was saying.

"Montana was here earlier, but that's none of your business."

"It is when she's gone missing."

"Missing? Where are the other girls?"

"Come on. Stop acting like you care. If you care, you wouldn't have had Major killed and your 'girls' terrorized in their own home."

"Whoever is behind this will pay."

Troy stood up. "Your fake concern might work with others, but I know the deal. You better not harm one hair on her head, or else you deal with me. Got it?"

Troy waited for a response. None came. Raymond was sobbing. "All I wanted to do is keep The Agency's reputation in tact. I worked too hard. We all worked too hard to build it. I told Major to leave it alone, but he wouldn't listen. Now it's come to this."

"You're good. I have to hand it to you," Troy stated.

"Montana. My sweet Montana."

"Look, what do you know about her disappearance?" Troy wasn't falling for the fake concern.

"We talked about her and her sisters. She told me how disappointed she was. I got called away. When I returned fifteen minutes later, she was gone."

"And that's it?" Troy asked.

"I've failed them. I've failed Major," Raymond stated.

"You killed him."

Raymond stood up and slammed his fist down on his desk, knocking some of the files on the floor. "Major got himself killed. I begged him to drop it, to go away quietly into retiring. Did he listen? No. Now things are getting all out of control." Troy listened to him go on and on. He hoped Raymond would reveal something he didn't know that would lead Troy to Montana.

"I love them like they were my own. No doubt about it. Why are we going back and forth? We need to find out what happened to Montana. Let's go look at the security tape."

Troy didn't trust Raymond, but he would play along with him until he could figure out what type of game he was playing.

~ 28 ~

Asia handed Savannah the phone. "Whoever it is insists on speaking with you only."

"Put it on speaker." Savannah walked closer to the phone so her voice could be heard. "This is Savannah."

"Back off, or else," a muffled male voice said.

"Who is this?" Savannah asked. She wrote on a piece of paper for Asia: *Call Troy.*

"Who I am isn't important. I have something you want."

Savannah was barely able to say her sister's name. She said, "Montana?"

"I heard you were smart."

Savannah was trying to remain cool, but she was on the verge of losing it. "Let me speak to her."

She heard what sounded like scuffling. "Vanna, I'm okay. It's—"

Before she could finish, the line went dead. Savannah released her breath and collapsed on the sofa. Asia walked back in. "Troy is on his way . . . with Uncle Raymond."

"What? I can't believe this. Montana's missing, and Troy's bringing the enemy into our house. Am I cursed?" Savannah wailed.

Asia ran to Savannah's side and they rocked in each other's arms. Savannah kept glancing at the phone, hoping the kidnapper would call back. Before long, the doorbell rang. Asia drew her gun. "Stay behind me," Savannah said.

Savannah motioned Asia to put her gun down. "It's Troy." She swung open the door.

"Any word?" he asked.

"No."

Uncle Raymond walked in behind Troy. He reached to embrace her; Savannah stepped back. His arms flew to his side. "It's been a misunderstanding, dear, and we need to talk."

Savannah fumed with anger. "How dare you? First you killed my dad, and now Montana."

Troy placed his arms around Savannah. "Breathe in and out. He's here to help."

Savannah jerked out of Troy's arms. "Traitor. How dare you side with him? After everything he's done."

Asia stood and watched the exchange. She didn't say a word. She stood with her arms folded.

They all stood at a standstill in the foyer in front of the front door. "Right now, everybody is a little emotional, so let's calm down so we can find Montana," Uncle Raymond said.

Troy said, "He's right. Let's all go sit down so we can figure out where Montana is." Troy reached out to touch Savannah's arm. She jerked it and strode into the living room.

Addressing Troy, Savannah pressed the button on the recorder. She watched her uncle as the kidnapper's voice played. He didn't flinch. She didn't expect him to. He was a master manipulator. She refused to fall for his show of kindness ever again. He was behind her dad's death, and he would go down with the rest of the people on the list.

Troy asked, "What do you think?"

Savannah couldn't believe Troy was asking Uncle Raymond for his advice. She felt like throwing the lamp at him.

Raymond said, "Whoever has her isn't going to harm her. Not right now, so that gives us some time."

Asia spoke up. "Of course you know that, because you know who has her."

Raymond looked between Asia and Savannah. "I am at a loss, just like you are. You girls mean everything to me."

"Tell that to someone who cares to hear the lies," Savannah snapped. She looked at Troy. "Although I'm pissed at you, I do value your opinion. What do you think about Montana's safety right now?"

"She's safe for the time being. But time might not be something we have on our hands. She was trying to tell you something, but the kidnapper disconnected the call. It sounds like she knows her abductor."

"He's sitting right here," Savannah stated with conviction.

"Vanna, I know you don't believe me, but you must trust me if we're going to get Montana back," Raymond said.

"You must think I'm crazy. There's no way in hell I'm going to trust you."

Raymond squirmed in his chair. "What I'm about to tell you is going to jeopardize everything, I know, but I'm willing to risk it if it means saving Montana," Raymond said.

Savannah crossed her arms. "Good ol' Unc."

Asia said, "Hush. I want to hear what he has to say."

"Fine," Savannah responded.

"It started a year before Major died. He confronted me right here. I tried denying it at first, but, of course, Major did his homework. He had dates and events that would not look too good if I went in front of a U.S. Senate committee . . ." Raymond's voice had trailed off as he told the chain of events that led up to Savannah's dad's death.

"So many of the crooks we're after were getting away free. My men were risking their lives to bring them in, and the courts were setting them free. I couldn't have it. I set up a unit whose sole purpose was to get to the enemy before the other division and eliminate them. Unfortunately, during the process innocent folks sometimes might have gotten hurt. Major didn't like the fact that we were twisting the law, but we've always done it. Maybe not with the intent of killing, but Bridges here could tell you how we always got our target, and by any means necessary."

"That doesn't explain why you had my dad killed," Savannah said, barely above a whisper.

All eyes went from her back to Raymond. "I warned Major that if it leaked that he knew more about this other unit, that it could jeopardize his life. I did my best to convince him to enjoy his retirement and to leave everything to me. But you know Major. Once he got an idea in his head, he wouldn't stop until . . . well, until I got a call from you all that someone had killed him." He paused before continuing. "I loved Major like a brother, and I did not have him killed. I know you don't believe me, but I didn't. I do know *why* it happened, but I haven't been able to figure out *who*. That's another reason why I didn't want you girls snooping. Whoever killed Major could be coming after you, if they think you know more than you've let on."

Savannah clapped her hands. "You're so good. Asia, hand him his Oscar."

Raymond stood up. "I guess the only way to prove to you that I didn't have anything to do with Major is to help you find Montana."

"That'll be a step in the right direction," Asia said.

Savannah couldn't believe Asia was falling for his lies. "Look, we need you to call whoever you have to call and get us our sister back here, alive and well. Pronto."

"I'll do what I can," Raymond said.

"That's not good enough. You need to promise me you'll get Montana back," Savannah snapped.

Troy attempted to calm her. "Savannah, he says he doesn't know where she is."

"Bull."

Troy turned to Raymond. "Do what you can on your end, and I'll use my contacts on my end. Call me on this number." Troy wrote down a number and handed it to him.

"Girls, it's going to be okay. Montana will be back, safe and sound."

Troy walked Raymond out.

Savannah was furious. "Can you believe the nerve of that man?" She cursed. "I bet you he planned this whole thing. Just so he could get back into our good graces."

Troy returned. "Savannah, I don't think he's behind Montana's disappearance. I looked at the tapes and she did get back in her car around eight fifty-nine. Alone."

"That doesn't mean anything. He could have called someone. I'm not buying it," Savannah said.

"I'm not ruling him out completely, but for now, we're working on the same team. For now, I won't have to worry about anybody trying to kill me, which means I can concentrate on you three."

Asia said, "Thanks, Troy, for your help. We really do appreciate you."

Savannah didn't say anything else. She walked away. She heard Asia say, "I don't trust Uncle Raymond either, but I do trust you. I just pray we don't live to regret it."

"You and I both," Savannah said as she headed upstairs to lie across her bed.

She needed to rest her nerves. Every time she closed her eyes, her thoughts replayed the conversation with the kidnapper. It replayed what Raymond had said. She cried out for her dad.

Troy heard her cries, and when he entered the room, without saying a word, he lay across the bed with her and cradled her in his arms. They stayed that way until the phone rang.

~ *29* ~

"That might be the kidnapper," Savannah said as she grabbed the phone and sat up on the side of the bed.

"I hooked up a tracing device on the phone, so keep them talking," Troy said. He raced downstairs so he could work the device, which was hooked up to his laptop.

Asia was viewing the computer screen. She moved out of the way when she heard him come in. "It says it's not connected," Asia said.

"She needs to keep him on for at least five minutes. If she does, we can lock it in."

Asia said, "I'll go make sure."

Troy placed his headphones on and listened in on the conversation as he watched the monitor. "Come on, you can do it," Troy cheered Savannah on.

The voice on the phone was muffled. He would need to take the tape home to see if he could remove the noises. "Do you know how long I've waited for this day?" the kidnapper asked.

Savannah responded, "All I care about is Montana. Whatever you want, we'll get it to you."

"You can't give it to me. Can you give me back my life?"

"Sir, if it's money you need, we can get it. Just tell us how much and where to bring it."

Troy's computer beeped. The alert locked in on a location. He zoomed in. He wrote down the address. "Asia," he yelled.

Asia ran back down the stairs. "Did you get it?"

Troy scribbled the address down. "Call Raymond. Tell him to meet me there."

"What do I tell Savannah? She's still on the phone with him."

"Good. Don't say a word until she's off the phone. Tell her I said that she did a good job."

Troy rushed out and almost ran over one of the neighbors as he rushed down the street. He called Dion. He could tell he was on the phone because of the way the phone beeped. "Pick up. Hurry up," Troy said.

"Any news?" Dion asked.

"I think I know where she is. I'm on my way there now. Can you meet me there?" he asked.

"What's the address?"

Troy gave Dion the address and sped to his destination. Dion must have been nearby because he was there before Troy arrived. Raymond was nowhere in sight. Dion was wearing plainclothes attire. *He must have been working outside* was Troy's first thought.

"I didn't go in, just in case there's more than one."

"Good thinking," Troy responded as he drew his weapon. "You back me up. If I'm not out in, say, fifteen."

"Gotcha."

Troy went around the building to see if he could locate any other vehicles. The only two vehicles were his and Dion's. He found an opening in one of the windows and slipped through, undetected. Once his eyes adjusted to the darkness, he went from room to room in what looked to be an abandoned warehouse. One of the rooms looked like it was being used for office space. "Doggone it," he said. He realized he was only minutes away from locating the kidnapper. The phone the culprit had used had been yanked out of the wall.

He picked up a locket that he recalled seeing around Montana's neck.

He called Dion. "All's secure. We just missed them."

"Man, my boss just called. I hate to run."

"No, go, man. Thanks. We'll be in touch," Troy said as he dialed Savannah.

"You did a great job. I don't know what happened, but it's as if he knew we were onto him."

Savannah said, "Had to be Uncle Raymond. He's the only other person besides us, who knew."

Troy saw Raymond and a few other people come his way. "Speaking of the Devil. Let me call you back. Call me if they call back. Okay, sweetheart?"

He didn't mean to use the term of endearment, but he couldn't take it back. In fact, he didn't want to take it back.

"Looks like they got away," Raymond said.

"Looks that way," Troy responded. He wasn't 100 percent sure about Raymond and Montana's kidnapping. He said, "I see you brought some backup."

"Wanted to be prepared, just in case," Raymond responded.

"Well, I need to get back to Savannah," Troy said. "And Asia."

Raymond said, "We need to get something understood first." Troy halted his step. Raymond continued talking. "What I told you back at Vanna's needs to stay there."

"That I can't promise you. But if it'll save Montana's life, I will do what I can," Troy said. He didn't wait for Raymond to respond.

He got in his vehicle and made it back to Savannah's in record time. He hoped that he wasn't underestimating the situation. Montana's life would depend on it.

The expression on Savannah's face when she opened the door made his heart skip a beat. She looked like she hadn't slept in days. Twenty-four hours ago things were as normal as they could be, under the circumstances. He wished he had insisted that they not leave his place.

"He called back. He said if I send the cops looking for him again, he's going to harm Montana." Savannah sobbed.

Troy wrapped his arms around her and held her until she felt comfortable letting him go. She led him into the makeshift command station.

"What I find strange is that he knew we were coming," Troy said as he retold the events.

Asia confessed, "I think it's Uncle Raymond. Actually, I'm hoping it's him, because I don't think he'll do anything to Montana. He probably just wants the disc."

Troy thought about it for a moment. "Maybe."

Savannah remained quiet the entire time. With her legs curled up under her, Savannah looked to be deep in thought. She said, "Call Uncle Raymond. Tell him that we have a disc Dad left. Give it to him and see what happens."

"No, we can't do that. That disc is important."

Asia pulled a disc out of her purse. "She didn't say the *only* disc. This should be enough to pacify him."

"Are you sure?" Troy asked.

"Yes. If it means getting Montana back, then I'll drop the whole thing. Well, at least make him think I'm dropping it."

Troy called Raymond. "The girls want to see you right away." He paused. "No, nobody's heard from him . . . They have a proposition . . . We'll be waiting."

Savannah asked, "What did he say?"

"He wanted to know if we had heard from Montana's abductor."

"Like he doesn't know the answer to that already," Asia said.

Savannah stood up and paced the floor. "Asia, let me do most of the talking. Your temper might give us away."

"You bet. The more I think about it, the more I want to bash his head in."

"I need to make some phone calls," Troy said.

"We're not going anywhere," Savannah answered.

"Ladies, hang on in there. We're going to get her back." Troy hoped he sounded confident. Right now, he wasn't so sure about her return, if they couldn't track down the kidnapper. He had worked on other kidnapping cases and knew time was of the essence. The longer it took to track down Montana's location, the less chances she would have to survive. If only the kidnapper would ask for something, he could arrange to knock him off during the drop-off. What made this kidnapping different from others? The abduction seemed personal, not money driven. The only person who had something to gain from this had to be Raymond Steel.

Raymond was at the door by the time Troy was finished with his phone calls. He hoped giving him the disc would be enough. His gut instincts, though, told him that it still wouldn't get Montana back. But he had to try, for Savannah's sake.

30

"Raymond," Savannah said.

"It's still Uncle," he responded.

Savannah handed him a disc in a glass case. "I think this is what your guys were looking for when they broke into my house."

Raymond looked at the disc. "What is this?"

"It's everything that my dad had on The Agency," Savannah responded.

Raymond reached to hug her. Savannah held her hand up to halt him. "This doesn't mean all is forgiven. In fact, with Montana missing, I just can't do this. You have your disc; now give me back my sister."

"I wish I could."

"We gave you the disc, and now you still want to play us," Asia said. She swung at Raymond. Savannah jumped in front of Asia, and she missed hitting Raymond by a few inches. Troy remained in his seat, observing.

"Girls, I am doing what I can to find Montana. In fact, I think we have a lead."

Troy made his presence known. "Maybe we should take this conversation in the back."

Savannah folded her arms. "No. If he knows something, we all need to know."

Raymond sat down on the couch while Asia and Savannah remained standing. "We got a few fingerprints off the phone and the chair. I have someone running an analysis now. I'm just waiting on the phone call."

Asia commented, "You're a trip. You must have taken up acting in school."

Savannah said, "Asia."

Asia turned away from them. "I'm just saying. Acting like he cares." She continued to mumble until she was out of hearing distance. She left the room.

Savannah sat in the chair facing Raymond. "You better hope they find something."

"I'm glad you trust me to handle this," Raymond said.

Savannah laughed. "Trust you. Please. Never again. I just have hope. Hope that Montana comes out of this unharmed."

Raymond's phone rang. He put his hand up to signal them all to be quiet. He answered. Savannah stood up and walked to the mantel. Troy walked up behind her. He started massaging her shoulders.

"Hey, you're handling this well," he whispered.

"I just feel so helpless," Savannah responded.

Raymond cleared his throat. "Excuse me. Don't mean to interrupt, but we have a few leads."

Troy stopped massaging Savannah. They both turned to face Raymond. Troy said, "What do you have?"

"My men are checking things out. Hopefully, we'll know something for sure in another hour."

"Troy, can you go work with his men? Please," Savannah pleaded.

Troy addressed Raymond. "You heard the lady. Give me the person's contact information who's in charge so I can go meet him."

"We got this," Raymond said.

Savannah responded, "If you want us to even consider that you had nothing to do with this, you will let Troy assist."

Raymond stopped to think for a moment. "I have nothing to hide. Troy, here's who you need to speak with." Raymond wrote some information down on a piece of paper and handed it to Troy. "I'll call to let them know you'll be helping."

Savannah sighed. "Thanks. I appreciate it."

"I'll do anything for you girls."

Asia had returned to the room and stood behind him, holding a cup of water. She was holding the cup so hard, it broke. Savannah was glad it wasn't glass.

Savannah walked Troy outside. "Do you think he's not telling us something?"

Troy hugged her and said, "I'll know for sure. Keep your phone near you."

"I will. Bring her home to me," Savannah pleaded.

Troy released her. "I'll do my best."

Savannah dragged herself back into the house. Troy was her only hope. She hadn't depended on a man since her dad, and she never thought she would have to depend on Troy or any other man for something like this.

She stood outside the front door and looked into the star-filled sky. For the first time since her Dad had died, she prayed sincerely to God. She prayed for forgiveness for all the thoughts that had run through her mind since her dad died. She prayed to God to protect her sister. For the first time since it all happened, she felt a calm come over her.

When she reentered the house, Asia was sitting on one side of the living room, and Raymond was sitting on the other side. It would be a long time before she ever would feel like calling him "Uncle" again. Whether he was guilty or innocent of Montana's disappearance, he was behind her dad's murder. She was confident of that. And for that, she could not forgive him. That was something she would have to ask God to help her with.

Raymond was the first to break the silence. "Come and sit." He patted the space next to him.

Savannah sat, but she sat in the chair across from him. She didn't trust herself not to reach out and hit him. It was for the best they kept their distance.

"The men I have on this are some of the best. Whoever has Montana will regret the day they thought of the idea," Raymond assured her.

"I hope you're right," Savannah said. She leaned back in her chair and folded her arms.

Savannah watched Asia leave the room. She didn't like it when Asia was silent. Asia was a very vocal person; her silence was frightening.

"As I was telling Asia while you were outside, I appreciate you giving me the disc. I know it'll take you a while to trust me again, but it's for the best."

Savannah leaned forward in her seat. "Don't think it's a done deal. Granted, you might not be behind Montana's kidnapping, but what you did to my dad is not forgivable. Once this situation here is cleared up, don't even think about being a part of our lives ever again."

"I know you're upset with what's going on, but think about this. I've been a part of your lives since you were little girls," Raymond said.

"And that's what hurts and makes this so difficult. But I cannot in good conscience live a lie—a lie that you obviously have been living out since last year. I'm not like you. I can't hide my transgressions."

"When it's all over, you'll see that I'm not as guilty as you think I am."

"Prove it now. Prove to me right now that you had nothing to do with my dad's murder and I'll apologize and make sure my sisters do too," Savannah challenged.

"In time, dear."

"Time . . . time . . . time . . . In time, you'll take the disc we gave you, make sure that you eliminate any threats to you, and then throw it in our faces and say, 'See, I told you.' Please. We're not as dumb as you think," Savannah said.

"I never said you were dumb. In fact, all of you have your dad's smarts. That's why I feel that wherever Montana is, she will survive. She's a fighter, and I feel for her abductor."

Raymond said the first thing Savannah could agree with. Montana was not going out without a fight. The only way the abductor was probably able to get her in the first place was catching her by surprise.

The phone rang, but the battery on the handset was out. Savannah rushed and answered the phone in the kitchen. Asia came in to let her know that she was using the tracing equipment. Raymond was trying to coach Savannah by writing things on a piece of paper.

Savannah was going to ignore him, but she thought better of it. The kidnapper now was demanding money.

Raymond wrote: *Ask him for a drop-off place and time.*

Savannah repeated what she read. The kidnapper gave her an amount and date. She had less than twenty-four hours to come up with a quarter of a million dollars. She had money in savings and stocks, but it would take time for the stocks to be sold and money deposited in her account to fulfill the kidnapper's request. She hung up the phone.

Raymond said, "I'll give you all the money you need."

Savannah felt relieved.

31

Savannah was all he could think about. Finding Montana was a top priority. He could not fail Montana or Savannah. The men he went to meet were checking out several leads. Thus far, everything came to a dead end. He had hoped to have something to report to Savannah by now. It had been two hours.

His phone vibrated. He answered. He listened to Savannah. "We have one more person to check out. I'm hoping this will be it."

Savannah said, "Be careful."

"Always," he responded before he disconnected the call.

He was disappointed that the last person on the list also led to a dead end. All he could do now was head back over to Savannah's and prepare to do the money exchange. Raymond might not be behind Montana's kidnapping—he was more confident about this now—but he would not go unpunished. The disc Troy still had in his possession would be enough to put Raymond and whoever else out of commission. Whether they did jail time or not, at least it would expose them for the crimes they committed. He would make sure the media wouldn't get all the gory details. He didn't want the men and women who were honestly doing their job and working in the field to be in jeopardy. He only wanted those who decided to take others' lives in their own hands, as if they were their Maker, to be held accountable.

Troy went home and picked up everything he thought they would need for tomorrow's drop-off. It had to be planned carefully, or it all could backfire. He packed up more surveillance equipment for Savannah to wear and for him to be able to set up remotely. Savannah would probably be watched when she left the house, so they would have to time things.

"Savannah, I'm outside," Troy said as he pulled into the driveway. Raymond's car was no longer there.

He rang the doorbell. It didn't take Savannah long to come answer the door. She hugged him as soon as he walked in. The smell of her perfume had his hormones on overload. He knew she was vulnerable with everything going on, so he would not take advantage of her. He wanted her to come to him when she was 100 percent sure of her emotions, not out of need for comfort.

His body was betraying him as she kissed him. The items in his hands slid to the floor as his willpower was getting weaker and weaker. "Vanna. I can't," he said in between kisses.

"I need you," Savannah begged.

Troy didn't want to disappoint her, but he didn't want her to have any regrets the next day either. "Baby, I want you more than anything, but not like this."

Savannah removed her arms from around his neck and pulled away. "Not even this is working out." She was sobbing.

His heart tugged. He was torn between doing the right thing and giving in to Savannah's emotional state. He had to do the right thing. He picked up the bags, which had slipped and fallen, and placed them on a table.

Savannah sat with her legs curled up under her in the chair across from the couch.

"Baby, you need to get some sleep. We have a long day ahead of us and you need to be well rested," Troy said.

"I can't sleep. I can't eat. Asia's not talking. I'm just all alone." Savannah began sobbing again.

Troy walked to where she sat and bent down on his knees. He took her face in his hands and pulled her head up. They were staring into each other's eyes. "As long as I'm alive, you'll never be alone." He kissed the tears streaming down her face. When their lips locked together this time, neither one pulled away.

Troy needed her as much as she needed him. "Let's go upstairs," Savannah suggested.

Troy stood up. "Savannah Blake, you've had my heart for what seems like forever. I love you, and because I love you, when I go up those stairs, it will be to hold you."

"But—"

He placed his index finger to her lips. "Shh, come on."

Instead of Savannah leading him to her room, Troy led her. He pulled back the covers of her bed. He undressed her with his eyes first before using his hands to do the work. With each piece of clothing he took off, his lips pressed on the body part. He unbuttoned her shirt. He kissed her on each shoulder as the shirt fell off. He used one of his free hands and unbuttoned her pants. He let the pants slide down. His lips traced her stomach all the way to her belly button. Savannah sighed with each kiss.

He lifted each leg and kissed between her thighs as he removed each pant leg. He gently led her to the bed. Before joining her in the bed, he put on a strip show of his own. He got excited seeing the desire in Savannah's eyes as he removed his clothes. He lay on top of her and kissed her, until both were moaning as if they had reached an orgasm. All of this happened without them having sexual intercourse.

Troy's reserve weakened with each touch, but in the end he did the right thing. He snuggled up with Savannah. "Good night, my sweet."

Savannah didn't protest this time. She responded, "Good night."

Troy could feel the rapid beat of her heart. As the stress left her body, the beat slowed its pace and her breathing became even. When Troy was confident she was sleeping peacefully, he closed his eyes.

When he woke up the next morning, Savannah's leg was wrapped around his body. His lower member was on high alert. He wanted to show her how much he loved her, and if Asia hadn't knocked on the door, he would have forgotten his promise to himself and to her to wait.

"Savannah! Troy's truck is outside, but I don't see him," Asia yelled. She attempted to turn the knob, but, thankfully, one of them had remembered to lock the door.

Troy nudged Savannah to wake up. "Asia's at the door."

"I'll be out soon," Savannah said without even opening her eyes.

"You're so cute when you sleep," Troy commented.

"Uh-huh. Wake me up later," Savannah said as she dozed back to sleep.

"Baby, we need to get the day started. There's a lot of stuff we need to go over," Troy said.

Savannah reluctantly pulled herself out of the bed.

Troy beat himself up for thinking logically. Savannah looked sexy in her purple-laced underwear. He was glad she didn't look back, because she would have seen him at attention. He tried to think of other things to calm his member down, but nothing worked. He waited for her to enter the bathroom before he got up and put his clothes back on. He went downstairs and outside to his truck. He brought in his overnight bag and a box with his other gear.

He used the downstairs bathroom to shower. Asia and Savannah were both downstairs when he exited.

"I know what you were doing," Asia teased.

Troy's mouth dropped open. He hoped she didn't know that he just relieved himself of the buildup of the tension he felt for not taking Savannah up on her offer. The guilt on his face said it all. Fortunately for him, Asia didn't press the issue.

"Anybody hungry?" Savannah asked. "For some reason I woke up with a healthy appetite."

Asia added, "I'm sure you did."

"What?" Savannah said innocently.

"You two are something else," Asia said.

"Asia, drive your car into the garage," Troy said.

"Why don't we go in your truck?" Savannah asked.

"No. Whoever the kidnapper is needs to see something familiar. I'm sure he knows your vehicles. Your Mustang is too small for what I need to do."

Asia followed his directions. While Savannah cooked, Troy set up the equipment in Asia's car. Asia assisted him with the wiring. "This should do it."

"I never would have thought to put a tracer on the car."

"It'll give us Savannah's location, just in case he decides to switch the drop-off location at the last minute. In the past it's happened more times than I can count."

After they ate a hearty breakfast, Troy went over the plans. "I don't know what Raymond has planned. Although I don't think he has anything to do with Montana's disappearance, I don't trust him."

"You can't be serious. I think he knows exactly where she is."

"Savannah, I've worked on cases like this before, and although he's a good actor, I honestly don't feel that he knows."

"If you say so," she responded.

"Raymond will have his men doing their thing, but we'll be doing our own. I'll set the wire up on you, and you do exactly what the kidnapper tells you. If he tells you to go to another location drop, do so. I have a tracer on your car."

Asia stated, "We'll be in Troy's SUV, so don't worry."

"He might even frisk you to see if you have any weapons," Troy said. He reached into the box and brought out a very small handgun.

"I didn't know they made anything that small," Savannah said, taking it from Troy's hand.

"He'll never detect this. Put this here." Troy moved his hand on her waistband. He noticed the concern on Savannah's face. "Don't worry. It won't go off unless you remove the safety. When someone does a pat search, it'll go undetected."

Asia said, "Why doesn't she just put it in her thirty-eight double-D chest? They definitely won't be able to find it there."

"Asia!" Savannah yelled.

"Well, you both know I'm telling the truth."

Troy looked at Savannah. "She does have a point."

"I am not putting this gun in between my breasts," she said, swinging the gun from side to side.

"Whoa, Annie Oakley. It's small, but still lethal," Troy said as he ducked away from Savannah's aim.

"I have a choice," Savannah joked. "If it goes off, I could either lose a boob or my side. Decisions. Decisions."

"Whatever you decide, do it quickly, because time is winding down."

Asia looked at the clock. "One o'clock couldn't come fast enough for me."

The doorbell rang. Troy went to see who was outside. "It's Raymond." He alerted them.

Raymond came in, giving orders. "Troy, I want you working with my men. Savannah, I'll ride with you. Asia, you stay here, just in case."

Troy didn't have to say anything because Savannah had it all under control. "Raymond, I appreciate everything you're doing, but I'm riding by myself," she contradicted.

Asia interjected, "And there's no way I'm staying behind with both of my sisters' lives in danger."

"It's for the best. I'm only thinking of your safety." Raymond looked at Savannah. "And you have no idea how these things can turn out. You take him the money, and he ends up killing you and her."

Troy said, "Speaking of money, Savannah said you were providing the cash. Where is it?"

"It's in my car. I'll be right back."

Savannah said a few obscene words. "Who does he think he is? He can't come in here trying to boss me. Ooh, if I didn't need that money, I would tell him to kiss my you know what."

Troy rubbed her shoulders. "We'll go with our original plan. Let me talk to him. We can use all the eyes we can get."

Raymond returned with a New Orleans Saints duffel bag. "This is two hundred and fifty thousand dollars. He won't get far, because there's a tracker at the bottom."

Asia picked up some of the money and let it fall on the table. "So this is how two hundred and fifty thousand dollars feel. I could sleep on this."

"Don't go getting too comfortable," Savannah said. She took the money from Asia's hand and placed it back in the duffel bag. She zipped it up and threw the bag on the floor. "Troy, tell Raymond our plan, so we can get this show on the road."

Troy could tell that Raymond wasn't too keen on their plan, but knew he had no choice from the look on Savannah and Asia's faces. He reluctantly agreed. He made a few phone calls and said, "It's a go. We're ready to move when you are."

32

Savannah went to the bathroom, and although everybody probably assumed she was using it, she actually went for some quiet time. Although Raymond and
Troy did this kind of drop-off thing all of the time, she
didn't. She was scared. She prayed until she heard the
knock on the bathroom door.

Troy's voice called from the other end, "It's time."

"Okay, I'll be out in a minute." She wiped her face with
a cold towel.

Everybody was waiting for her in the kitchen. "I'll be
fine," she said.

She placed the tiny handgun on her side, picked up
the duffel bag full of money, and went to her car.

Troy said, "We won't be far behind. Raymond has
some men set up at the first drop-off. But I'm sure
that's just a test to see if we're going to follow. Asia
and I won't be far behind. If you get a second drop-off
point, I want you to repeat it so Asia can write it down,
okay? Everything you do, you need to make sure you
verbally repeat it . . . but don't be too obvious."

Savannah sighed. "Got it."

She turned the radio on but heard Troy's voice in her
ear. "The music drowns out the sounds."

Savannah responded, "Sorry." She turned the radio
down and drove to her destination. She looked in her
rearview mirror to see if she was being followed. She
saw Troy and Asia a few cars behind her. She knew they

would soon drop off. It was like Troy was reading her mind.

"I don't see anybody following us. Raymond is meeting his men at their locations, so chill out, dear. We got your back."

Savannah smiled. She drove on in silence. She could hear the tires' movement on the road. Each sound was magnified. The cars screeching and horns blowing seemed to be louder than normal. Music usually calmed her; instead, she took deep breaths in and out to calm herself.

She arrived at the busy park at precisely twelve fifty-five. Five minutes before the official drop-off. She looked around to see if she saw any suspicious behavior. Women were playing with their kids. Men and women sat talking. A few people were there by themselves, reading books and magazines. Some were walking their dogs, or the dogs were walking them, depending on how you looked at it.

One o'clock approached, and she checked her phone to make sure the ringer was on. She exited the car and stood by it, as previously instructed. She waited to hear further instructions. A little boy threw a ball in her direction. She bent down to retrieve it, and was about to throw the ball back at him, but the child ran out of sight. In those few seconds her attention was brought back to the ball, and that's when she saw the message scribbled on it.

Go to the trash can. She read the note a few times. She looked around. No one seemed to be out of place. She got something out of her car, acting as though she was going to throw something away. There was a small envelope with her name on it in the trash can. She picked it up, but she waited until she was back in the car before she opened it to read.

She made sure she spoke out loud. "'To be on the safe side, I decided to change the location. Meet me at the outlet mall in Grapevine. Once there, go to the information booth. Ask for directions to Gonzales. Your instructions will be left there in a pamphlet.'"

Savannah threw the note down. She wanted to scream, but she didn't want to bring more attention to herself. Troy spoke in her earpiece. "I know you're probably frustrated, but we can catch him still. No worries. Okay, kid? We'll meet you at the outlet."

Savannah thought she was going to be stopped for speeding, but both times the police officers only waved at her to signal her to slow down. She did slow down, but as soon as they were outside her view, she sped up.

She didn't see Troy, or anyone else, but she couldn't wait for them to arrive. She exited the car and went to the information booth, as instructed. The clerk handed her a pamphlet. She wondered if the clerk was working with the kidnapper. She didn't open the pamphlet until she was a few feet away. It read: *Glad you came alone. Meet me on the pier in fifteen minutes.*

She hoped Troy was able to hear her over the background noise of the people talking in the outlet mall. She didn't get a response in her ear. She took the duffel bag and pretended to be window-shopping. She walked toward the pier. She looked over her shoulders at every sound. *I have to calm down. Montana's life could depend on it,* she thought.

Savannah tried to ease her fears by breathing in and out. She could sense that Troy was near, even before he voiced it through her earpiece. "I'm in the mall. Asia and I both are wearing hats. Don't fear, baby. We got your back."

Savannah let out the sigh she had been holding in.

Before she realized it, someone had something stuck in her back. "Keep on walking. Act normal. We're going to take a walk up that way," the voice said. Savannah recognized that voice, but she couldn't remember from where. She didn't resist. She did as instructed.

"Where's my sister?" Savannah asked.

"You'll see her soon enough," he responded.

Where was Troy? Where was her Uncle Raymond? That was all Savannah could think about as they were walking to a remote area of the pier. She had no idea that the building was on the end. She had never walked that far out.

"Don't turn around. Hand me the duffel bag. Montana is in the boat," the man said.

Savannah was about to turn around to hand him the money and he shouted, "No! If you turn around, I won't be able to let you leave."

"Here. Now go get my sister."

"You have less than ten minutes. If you don't get to her, she'll drown."

Savannah dropped the duffel bag and ran down the pier. She climbed the stairs that led to a boat. Water was creeping on the boat. She heard something move. She was relieved to see Montana, who was tied up and had something over her mouth. Savannah looked around to see if anyone was coming to help. Where were they? Time wasn't on her side; the boat was sinking. She tried to untie Montana, but without any good results. She removed the tape covering her sister's mouth.

"Vanna," Montana's weak voice said.

Savannah said, "Shh, I'm going to get you out of here."

Montana opened her mouth to say something but fainted.

Asia yelled, "Vanna! Where are you?"

"Down here!" Savannah responded.

Asia rushed down the stairs to the boat. "Help me get her up," Savannah cried out.

Asia and Savannah were able to get Montana off the boat, and Savannah barely had her foot on the last step before the little boat sank.

Raymond rushed over and pulled out a knife and cut the rope. He picked Montana up and rushed her to where some paramedics were waiting.

They paced in front of the ambulance until Montana came to. The medic had placed an oxygen mask over her mouth and nose, so she wasn't able to talk. The tears streaming down Montana's face tore at Savannah's heart.

"She's going to be all right, isn't she?" Savannah asked the medic.

"Yes. She's a little dehydrated and probably in shock from the cold water. We need to get her to the nearest hospital."

"I'm riding with the ambulance," Asia said.

For the first time Savannah thought to ask about Troy. "Where's Troy? I didn't see him."

"He tackled the kidnapper. I don't know where he is. I rushed to find you," Asia responded.

"He'll have to catch up with us later. I'm just relieved to have Montana back." Asia and Savannah hugged.

"We have to go," the medic responded.

"What hospital? Just in case I get lost," Savannah inquired.

"Metro," the driver replied.

"Savannah, wait, we need to ask you some questions," Raymond said.

"Not now, you don't." She walked around him and rushed to her car.

She tried her best to keep up with the ambulance but wasn't able. They were inside the hospital by the time she pulled up. She parked the car in a zone marked NO PARKING because she didn't have the time to wait for an available spot. She would deal with the ticket later.

Asia met her at the entranceway. "They say she's going to be okay, but I'm still worried," Asia said as they rushed to the emergency desk.

"We need one of you to fill out these papers so we can admit her," the hospital attendant said.

"I'll do this. Asia, you go check on her," Savannah stated.

After what seemed like an hour, but was only five minutes, Savannah filled out the form as best as she could. Some of the things she left blank. The attendant seemed to be moving in slow motion as she entered the data in the computer system.

"I don't mean to seem ungrateful, but I really must go check on my sister. My contact number is on there, which is my cell phone, if you need anything else."

Savannah didn't wait for her to respond. She went in search of Montana. She was in one of the makeshift rooms in the emergency area. Asia sat by the bed, holding her hand.

"The nurse said she's going to be fine. They gave her something to sleep," Asia said.

"What about the doctor? Has he been in here yet?" she asked.

"Not that I know of."

Savannah left the room and went to the nurses' station. "My sister was kidnapped and is suffering from shock, or God knows what. I need a doctor in her room ASAP!"

The head nurse stood up. "Calm down, miss, or we will have to ask you to leave."

"I'm not going anywhere until a doctor sees about my sister."

"Baby, baby, I got this," Troy said as he entered through the door.

Savannah watched Troy pull out his wallet, but she couldn't hear what he told the nurse. A few minutes later she was on the intercom paging a doctor.

Troy wrapped his arm around her and led her away. "It's going to be all right," Troy said.

"Where were you? Montana could have drowned in that boat. I could have drowned," Savannah said. She didn't want to seem ungrateful, but the stress was catching up to her. He was the closest thing to her, so he would feel the brunt of her frustrations.

"I was watching you. We couldn't play our hand or the kidnapper would have bolted. In fact—"

Before Troy could finish, a doctor came around the corner and headed toward Montana's room. Savannah grabbed his hand. "It's about time."

They stood to the side as the doctor examined Montana. She was still out of it and was barely coherent.

"How long will it take for the medicine to wear off?" Troy asked.

"She'll be like this until tomorrow morning," the doctor responded. He turned toward Savannah and Asia. "She's going to need plenty of rest. Her body went into shock being in the water. I understand she was a kidnap victim. We have counselors on staff who can help her with dealing with the aftermath," he suggested.

"Thank you, Doctor," Savannah responded.

He pulled out several business cards from his pocket and handed one to each sister. "If you need anything, don't hesitate to call me."

Savannah laid her head on Troy's chest. He held her. Asia sat down and leaned back. Savannah was glad to have both of her sisters safe and sound.

~ 33 ~

"Let's talk. But not in here," Troy said.

Savannah and Asia followed him to the crowded break room. They found a couple of seats near the back. The chairs weren't meant to be comfortable, but they would do. "The man who kidnapped Montana was taken into custody."

"Thank God," Savannah said.

"But it's not over," Troy added.

Asia said, "Did he escape?"

"According to him, he was hired by his brother."

Savannah and Asia looked at each other. Raymond was an only child, so that ruled him out. "I'm lost," Savannah said.

"He's Dion's brother," Troy blurted out.

"No way," Asia said as she looked to be digesting the information.

"That can't be right. Dion? Montana's ex? Your friend Dion?" Savannah repeated.

"Yes, sweetheart," Troy said.

"Why?" Asia asked.

"That's what we're trying to figure out," Troy said.

"I'll kill him," Savannah said. Her hands were shaking.

"He's a cop. He's not a kidnapper. His brother must be on drugs," Asia said. She kept trying to justify why Dion wasn't the culprit.

Troy said, "Listen. Dion was obsessed with Montana. According to his brother, when your dad made him break up with her, he ended up marrying that woman he cheated with. Well, I can fill in some of the blanks, because we were in the service together. Well, anyway, fast-forward a few years. His ex-wife cheated on him and ended up giving him HIV."

Savannah's mouth dropped open. "What?"

"A part of him blamed Montana. He took this opportunity—an opportunity that I regret I gave him by getting him involved with all of this. . ." Troy's voice trailed off as he considered his actions.

Savannah snuggled her body closer to his and said, "It's not your fault. We don't blame you. Do we?" Savannah looked at Asia.

Asia didn't say anything at first, but then said, "No, we don't blame you. We just blame that lunatic, Dion."

"Where is he now?" Savannah asked.

"That's the thing. Nobody knows. We don't know if he knows we have his brother or not. We're not allowing him to make any phone calls."

"I have a plan," Savannah said. Troy gave her his undivided attention. "Why don't I call him? Tell him we found her, but she's in a coma. If I can lure him to the hospital, maybe he'll do something stupid."

"It could get dangerous, and I don't want you risking your life ever again," Troy said.

"We have to do something. What if Montana would have died?" Asia countered.

Troy said, "Dion has no idea that his brother was asking for ransom. I hate to tell you this, but Montana's not supposed to be in there. She's supposed to be—"

Savannah put her hand up. "Don't say it."

"Now you see why I don't want you calling him. I have a few of my men and Raymond's looking for Dion."

"I'm sure he knows that. He's not going to suspect us. Let me call him," Savannah said.

Asia added, "Let's get Montana in another room. I'll dress up as her and lay out. He'll come in the room thinking it's her all by herself. You guys be in the bathroom. If he does anything stupid, you jump him."

Savannah said, "I like the plan, except it'll be me pretending to be Montana, instead."

They looked at Troy. "Hey, I don't agree with either plan, so I'll leave that decision up to y'all."

"I'm doing it. Decision made," Asia said as she stood up.

"Fine. But if anything happens, it's on your head," Savannah snapped. Savannah stood up to get a better signal on her cell phone. She dialed Dion's number.

Troy and Asia overheard her end of the conversation. From the sound of it, Dion fell for the bait. "Okay, Troy, move Montana to a safe spot. Asia, let me do some stuff. I'm not as good as Montana, but hopefully, I can make you look like a victim."

"Don't be so enthusiastic about it," Asia said.

Troy found a vacant room and moved Montana to it. He made sure that if a person was to walk down the hall, he would not be able to see who was in the bed. Troy was amazed at Asia's transformation when he entered Montana's hospital room. "I don't even want to ask. The thing over the head is a good idea, because all of you have different hairstyles."

"I'll take credit for it," Asia said.

"Savannah, I'll be in the bathroom. You pretend to leave Dion alone with Montana."

"Got it. He should be here soon."

Troy was barely in the bathroom when Dion strolled through the door. Savannah was wearing a hidden camera. Troy got a good view of the room. Dion walked in, carrying an arrangement of flowers. "Thank God she's all right," he said, hugging Savannah before placing the flowers on the counter. "Has she come to yet?"

"No, the doctor said she's in shock. They don't know how long it'll be before she regains consciousness," Savannah stated.

"I wish I could get my hands around who did this," he said.

Troy heard Savannah say, "Me too." Troy prayed she wouldn't show her hand too soon.

Dion held Asia's hand. "I'm here. I wish I could make up for what I did to you"—he paused before continuing—"what I did to you so many years ago."

Savannah stood up. "Now that you're here, I want to go to the cafeteria and get something to drink."

"I can do it," Dion volunteered.

"No. You being here might make her wake up sooner. The doctor says it's good to talk to her. That she can hear us."

Savannah walked out of the room.

Troy waited and watched. Dion looked back to see if he was alone. He closed the door. He walked back to Montana's hospital bed. "You know I regret having to do this. I loved you. I loved you more than anything else in this world. If you live, my life is over." Dion let out a sinister laugh. "Who am I kidding? My life is already over. That trick I was married to gave me AIDS. I have a death sentence. Do you know how it made me feel when she told me she had given me the virus? I wanted to blow her head off right then. Instead, I watched her die a slow and painful death."

He removed a syringe from his pocket. "I should have wooed you. Made you fall in love with me. Slept with you without a condom, but instead I'll just prick myself and then prick you. Nobody will be the wiser.

I hope you enjoyed your life without me, because you will have a reminder of me from now on."

Before he could complete his act, Troy pounced on him. Asia rolled out of the bed from the other side and hit the floor while they struggled. Troy knocked the needle out of Dion's hand. The scuffle must have been loud enough to get Savannah's attention, because she reentered the room, but not by herself. Two police officers rushed in behind her.

"Sir, we advise you to be still, or we will have to Taser you," one of the officers said.

"I'm a cop! He's the one you need to be arresting," Dion yelled.

The other officer placed the handcuffs on Dion. "You have the right to remain silent. Anything you say—"

"Idiots, he attacked me."

Troy said, "Man, give it a rest. I would suggest you save all of that for your lawyer. Trust me, you're going to need one."

Dion tried to charge him. Savannah tripped him and kicked him on his back. "That's for my sister."

The police officers had on protective gear, since they knew he was HIV positive. Dion finally left the room without a fight.

One of the officers said, "It's cops like him that give us a bad name. Ma'am, you won't have to worry about him bothering you or anybody for a long time."

~ *34* ~

Savannah felt like a load had been lifted off her shoulders when the police escorted Dion out of the room. She hugged Asia. Asia said, "I was this close from using that handgun of yours and blowing his balls off. I just didn't want blood to splatter on me."

"You did the right thing," Troy assured her.

"Let's go check on our sister," Savannah said.

They followed Troy to the room where Montana was being kept. "You two can go home. I think I'm going to spend the night," Savannah said.

"Now, you know I'm not going anywhere," Asia said.

Troy intervened before an argument could occur. "Why don't you take shifts? There's a bed over there. One can sleep, while the other sits up."

Savannah hugged him. "What would I do without you?"

Troy smiled. "Let's hope you never have to find out, sweetheart."

"You two are sickening. Just admit you like each other, and get it over with already," Asia said with a pout.

"Please do," Montana said between coughing.

They rushed to her side. "We didn't mean to disturb you," Savannah said, holding Montana's hand.

"I'm okay. Just feel like I got hit by an eighteen-wheeler, but other than that, I'm just fine." Montana was back asleep before anyone could respond.

Troy said, "She'll be in and out like that, probably until tomorrow. She's going to be fine."

Savannah walked Troy to the door. "Thank you for everything. Because of you, Montana's back with us, safe and sound."

"I wish I could take the credit. This was all you. You handled it like a pro, baby."

"It's still hard to believe Dion was blaming Montana for him getting AIDS. Just crazy."

"People have killed for less," Troy said. "Sorry."

"No, I know what you mean." Savannah kissed him on the cheek. "Get some rest. I'll call you tomorrow."

"I don't want to leave you," Troy said.

"We're fine. The main threat is in jail, and I don't think Raymond is going to be doing us any more harm, now that he has that disc."

Troy hugged her and whispered in her ear, "Take care, my sweet."

Savannah and Asia took turns sleeping in the bed. It was hard to rest, because by the time either dozed off, a nurse was entering the room and checking on Montana. Before long, they both sat up in the chairs in the room, dozing off when they could.

Montana seemed to be in better spirits the following morning. After having eaten a full breakfast, she was perky. "I hope the doctor lets me out of here. I just want to get home," she said. "No offense, Savannah, but I've enjoyed our bonding at your place, but I'm talking about *my* home. I miss my cushy bed."

"No offense taken. I wish our lives could go back to the way they were," Savannah confessed.

Asia said, "I'm blessed. I know I don't tell you all enough, but I love you. I love you both."

"Group hug," Montana said.

They got up and hugged each other.

"Just what I like to see," Raymond said as he entered the room. He was carrying a bouquet of balloons marked GET WELL.

Savannah and Asia moved out of the way. They watched the exchange while sitting.

"Baby girl, I'm glad you're all right," Raymond said after he leaned down and kissed Montana on the cheek.

"Me too, Uncle Raymond." He handed her the balloons.

"Thanks."

Savannah took the balloons and tied them to a chair. Raymond stood over Montana. "Will you ever forgive me?"

Although he was looking at Montana, Savannah felt like he was talking to all of them. Montana responded, "I appreciate the balloons, but I think it's best that you leave."

"I will do whatever it takes to make it up to you girls," Raymond said.

Savannah went and stood by the door. "You can't bring us our dad back."

Raymond held his head low. "Call me if you need anything." When he got close to Savannah, he said, "I mean it. I do love you girls."

"Bye, Raymond," Savannah said, staring him in the eyes without blinking.

He waved at Asia and Montana, looked at Savannah one last time, and walked out. Savannah closed the door behind him. It made a loud thud.

Montana moved her bed so it would sit straight up. "He might have helped you guys, but he's still a snake."

"My sentiments exactly."

Someone knocked on the door. "Come in," Savannah said.

Troy entered with a white teddy bear holding a rose. "Hi, ladies. Guess who I ran into?"

"Unfortunately, we know already."

"I brought you a little something," Troy said.

Montana took the teddy bear and admired it. "It's so cute. Thanks, Troy."

"I'm jealous," Savannah teased.

Montana was released from the hospital later that afternoon. Savannah insisted on Montana staying with her. Montana protested, but the doctor only agreed to release her into the care of Savannah. Asia entertained Montana as Savannah cooked them a nice dinner.

"This is to my sisters," Savannah toasted. They held up their glasses of juice.

Savannah was curious to learn more about what had happened, but didn't want to pressure Montana. She knew that what Montana experienced was tragic, and could leave some emotional scars.

"Do y'all want to know something?" Montana asked. "The whole time I was tied up, I kept thinking about you all. About what Dad had taught us. I never gave up hope. I knew if I would have given up hope, I would be dead now," Montana said.

"You don't have to talk about it, if you don't want to," Savannah said.

"If I don't talk about it now, I'll explode."

Asia sat down on the floor in her favorite position. Savannah tucked her legs under a throw cover, because she was a little cold. Montana began to explain to them what had happened two days before.

"After I left Uncle Raymond's office, I had a breakfast date with Dion."

"Why didn't you tell us?" Asia asked.

"I was embarrassed. After insisting that I had no feelings for the dude, I didn't want to be made a fool of, in case things didn't work out between us."

Savannah couldn't believe what she was hearing. "I wouldn't have judged you."

"Yeah, right. Anyway, I met him at his place, like he told me to. In fact, if you guys go to his house, my car is probably still there now. He had a few sandwiches from Jason's Deli and some sweet tea. Y'all know how I love tea. The tea had a funny taste, so I didn't drink it all. I started getting woozy. By the time I realized I had been drugged, it was too late. I was tied up to a bed and couldn't move. I was a little disoriented at first. When I came to, I yelled my butt off. When he realized I wasn't going to be quiet, he put tape around my mouth. I'm so glad now that I didn't bite him, because, Lord knows, I still would be at the hospital for the insane because I couldn't live with thinking I had AIDS."

"Montana."

"I'm serious. I listened to him tell me how Dad threatened him to leave me alone. He said the only way he knew to get me to be finished with him was to cheat on me. He planned for me to catch him cheating. Well, you know the rest. His brother didn't want to help him out with the kidnapping, but Dion threatened to set him up and have him arrested again. His brother was afraid of going back to prison."

"This time he'll have company," Asia said.

"Do you know his brother said that Dion was going to kill me? I talked his brother into offering me up for ransom."

"The jerk," Asia said.

"I'm so glad I didn't marry him. He's a nutcase."

"And to think you would have had little nuts running around here calling me 'Aunt Asia.'"

Montana threw a pillow at Asia. Asia blocked it from hitting her face. They laughed and talked for the rest of the evening.

35

Troy was disturbed about the entire Dion situation. He couldn't imagine having to live with HIV or AIDS, but he knew in his heart that he would not go to the extreme that Dion had gone. It wasn't Montana's fault that he had it. *I guess living with a death sentence around your neck can make you snap,* Troy thought. He would like to think he would still do the right thing, and that he wouldn't try to bring pain to anybody else.

"Hi, Cheryl," Troy said as he exited the elevator.

"Hey, stranger. Oh, you have a visitor."

"I thought my calendar was clear," Troy responded before entering his office.

"It was, but he insisted that he wait."

"Early bird catches the worm, and you're not early," Raymond said.

"What are you doing here?" Troy asked.

"Here I thought our differences were water under the bridge."

"It would be if you weren't sitting in a chair in my office, breathing up air in my space."

"Business is good, I hear."

"No complaints." Troy hung up his coat and took a seat behind his desk.

"I wanted to thank you personally for helping out with the Montana situation."

"There's nothing I wouldn't do for Savannah or her sisters. But I know they aren't the real reason why you're here, so spit it out."

"You seem to have a top-notch operation going on over here. The Agency could outsource some assignments your way. We'll both come out winners."

"Raymond, come on now. You should know better than anyone that after everything that has gone down, I don't want anything to do with The Agency."

Raymond stood up. "If you change your mind, you know how to reach me. But I'll be honest with you, the offer might not stay on the table too long."

"I'm going to lose some sleep knowing that," Troy said as he leaned back in his chair.

"Think about it." Raymond walked toward the door, but before he opened it, he turned and said, "About the other situation. That's dead, correct?"

Troy was not going to play his hand. He smiled. "What situation?"

"That's what I thought. Good day, son." Raymond walked out.

"I'm not your son," Troy said as he got up and closed the door. He hit the intercom button on his phone. "Cheryl, hold all of my calls."

Cheryl was in his office before he could click the button off. "Who was that, and why do you have an attitude?"

"Slow down on the questions. That was my ex-boss, and I got work to do, as do you."

"A little touchy. I'll leave you alone for now, but if you need to talk."

"I'm fine," Troy assured her.

When Cheryl left, he called Savannah. After talking to her for about ten minutes, he felt better. Troy realized that his and Savannah's relationship had crossed the line a long time ago. He knew there was no going back to the way things were before. He had never felt this way about any other woman. He had been in lust with many, and had cared about many, but the feelings he had for Savannah never went away. He didn't know if he should act on it. He feared her rejection more than anything. When all of this was over, would she still want to see him, or was their time together numbered?

He met with his staff and got an update on their cases. His mind was on Savannah as he exited the parking lot. He decided that his company would go into more corporate security. If he was going to build a life with Savannah, he had to rethink some things, and that would be the first step. Granted, he would miss the excitement. Who was he fooling? He had some serious thinking to do. Savannah had him rethinking his way of doing business. Was she worth it? What if he pursued her and she turned him down? Just because she wanted to sleep with him didn't mean she wanted a long-term commitment. Could she forgive him for what happened in the past?

Troy's mind was filled with thoughts of Savannah and his job. He failed to realize he was being followed. The car behind him rear-ended him. Troy jolted. The car came again at top speed, so he knew immediately it wasn't an accident. He looked in his rearview mirror but couldn't make out the driver.

Troy dialed Savannah's number. "Have Asia look this up. Louisiana plates Alpha-Dog-Three-Six-Five-One."

"What's going on?" Savannah asked.

"I'm being followed. I need to know who they are, and then do me a favor. When we hang up, call the police and tell them I'm on Interstate 20 and I'm near the Lancaster exit."

He kept driving, trying to avoid hitting other cars. Savannah called him back. "The cops are sending someone in your direction. Asia says the plates come back private and it won't allow her access."

"Okay. Well, I need to concentrate. I'll call you when it's over."

"Troy," Savannah said.

"Yes," he said.

"I love . . ."

Troy didn't hear the rest of what she said, because the car bumped him and his cell phone went flying across the seat.

He hit a switch and his truck went into turbo mode. He dodged in between cars as much as he could. He took the next available exit. He looked in his rearview mirror and could not shake the person in the car behind him.

He abruptly stopped his car and prepared for the crash. Troy closed his eyes and thought pleasant things. His sudden stop surprised the other driver and they rammed right into his truck. Troy felt the impact as the air bag deployed.

Troy grabbed his gun and exited the truck. He rolled to the ground, prepared to shoot. The driver of the other car was lying on the side of the road. He checked his pulse. Troy knew from how his body was tangled, he was a goner. "No seat belt," he said out loud.

Sirens could be heard in the distance. A motorist stopped to assist. "We can just wait for the cops," Troy said.

He looked at his SUV. The back was totaled. "Sir, do you mind if I use your phone to call my girlfriend?" Troy asked.

"No, I don't mind. You sure you're okay? Your head's bleeding a little," the concerned motorist said.

Troy hadn't realized it. He looked at his reflection in the car's window. "I'll be all right."

He dialed Savannah's number. He assured her he was fine. "No, I'll have the tow truck or an officer drop me off at home . . . I do have other vehicles I can drive."

He got off the phone to speak with the cops and emergency personnel who had arrived on the scene. After he had been checked out by a medic, he was free to go with the tow truck driver. He soaked in the tub as soon as he got situated at home.

Savannah called to check on him several times that night. She wanted to come to him but was torn between visiting him and leaving Montana's side. Troy wished she would come to him, but he knew that was selfish. Montana needed her more than he did; well, that's what he told himself, anyway.

He was dozing off when his alarm alerted him that someone was at the end of his driveway. When he saw the red Mustang, his heart flipped. He buzzed Savannah in. He met her at the door and they shared a warm embrace.

"Asia insisted that I come. She was tired of me moaning," Savannah said. She looked him over to make sure he was okay. She noticed the bandage on his forehead.

"It's just a little scratch. The medic put some ointment on it so it wouldn't get infected."

Troy led her upstairs without either one saying another word. The music of their hearts played in the background as their lips touched. Savannah's hands roamed Troy's chest. He hoped she couldn't tell that his stomach was full of butterflies. He was an experienced lover, but Savannah made him feel like a virgin schoolboy. He let her hands explore his body. When he couldn't take it anymore, he removed her clothes, kissing her skin as he did.

The moans seeping from her lips were the incentive he needed to continue. Savannah stood before him naked. He inhaled her beauty with his eyes. This time when their lips locked, memories from their past overwhelmed him. Savannah fell on the bed. His kisses started from her neck as he worked his way down to her secret treasure. He went treasure hunting and was rewarded with a sound that he had missed, and had thoroughly enjoyed.

He fumbled in his drawer for a condom. Savannah skillfully placed it on him, and when their bodies united, it was as if the world stood still. Savannah looked into his eyes and he saw tears forming. He wanted to reach down and wipe them, but he couldn't because he was so engulfed in her that the volcano eruption from within wouldn't allow him to do anything but release. For those moments of pleasure they were as one. She was his missing link.

Troy kissed Savannah on the top of her forehead. "I love you."

Savannah snuggled her body closer into his. She responded, "I love you too."

Sleep was peaceful for both of them.

36

"Isn't this cozy?" Savannah heard a strange man say. Was she having a nightmare? Didn't she and Troy make mad, passionate love the night before? Why wasn't she having sweet dreams?

Savannah opened her eyes and swore she was looking into the eyes of Satan himself. There standing by the bed was a bearded man with beady black eyes. What really stood out to her was the black gun pointed straight at her. Troy was sound asleep. She nudged him with her elbow.

"What, baby? Let's sleep in," Troy said without waking up completely.

"Troy, we have company."

As soon as she said that, Troy jolted up in the bed.

The man holding the gun said, "Slow down, play-boy."

Savannah's body shook. Troy used his hand to comfort her.

"Don't make any sudden moves or she's a goner," the goon said.

"What do you want?" Troy asked.

"It's too late for asking questions. Get up," he said.

Troy was still naked, so the intruder got an eyeful when he got out of bed.

"You too."

Savannah looked at Troy. Troy shook his head no.

"She doesn't have any clothes on. At least give her time to put on some clothes."

"She's a cutie. I might need to tap that myself."

Before that, Savannah was scared, but when he said those words, he pissed her off. She wasn't about to show him her body. He would have to shoot her.

"Pass me my clothes, will you, honey?" she said to Troy. She tried to sound calm, although her heart was beating a mile a minute.

Troy looked at the goon. His head motion gave him the okay. Troy held the comforter up while she slipped on her clothes. Just as she had hoped, the small weapon had not fallen out of her pocket. She would wait for the right opportunity to surprise the person who had interrupted what was supposed to be a perfect morning with her lover.

Savannah slipped out of the bed. Troy reached down to put on his clothes.

The goon said, "No funny business, or both of you are dead. Troy, the boss wants you alive. I'll have to call and say we're bringing a guest."

He pointed the gun at them. "Let's go downstairs. You—you go first. I'll keep the girl in back, just in case you want to try some funny business."

Savannah felt the gun in the arch of her back. It wasn't a good feeling at all. Troy walked down the stairs with her and the goon close behind.

"Sit down over there," the goon said.

Both sat on the couch as he watched them before he pulled out his cell phone. "I got him. He was not alone . . . Yeah, her." He turned his back for a few seconds.

"I got a gun," Savannah whispered.

Troy said, "Give it to me."

Savannah answered, "No."

Troy's eyes alerted her that the goon's attention was back on them.

"No talking," he said to them, then turned his attention back to his call. "Yes. You say bring her too. Will do." He hung up the phone.

"Missy, it's your lucky day. Seems like the boss wants you two alive. Bet you wish you wouldn't have picked up this stray."

Savannah was amazed that Troy was able to hold his temper. He was far better than she was. She wanted to shoot the guy. She lifted her hand to do so, when Troy's hand held her arm. Her eyes pleaded with him to let her do it, but he shook his head no.

Troy took a chance on the goon saying something, he whispered, "Let's see who his boss is. I got you covered."

Savannah wasn't too sure about Troy's plan, but she trusted him.

Troy said, "Man, this is between me and whoever your boss is. This lady has nothing to do with it."

"If she doesn't come, I'll have to kill her. She's seen my face. You know the rules. Leave no witnesses."

Savannah said, "I promise I won't remember a thing. I have a family. My little girl," she lied.

The goon acted like he was having second thoughts. "No, you're coming along for the ride too. In fact, I'm through talking to you. Get up."

Troy and Savannah stood up and walked toward where he stood. Savannah said, "Your mama must be real proud of you."

"Shut up, trick," he responded.

Troy said, "Show some respect."

"Bridges, you're not in any position to be giving out demands . . . Hurry it up," he said.

Savannah thought that he had to be the dumbest person. If he knew anything about Troy, Troy was the one that others feared. If they didn't, they wouldn't be so bent on trying to take him down.

Although her nerves were on edge, she, too, wanted
to know who this man's boss was. Her instincts told her
his boss would be the man who had killed her dad. Now
justice would be served. It amazed her how he could tie
up Troy and keep the gun pointed in her direction at
the same time. Savannah contemplated on taking aim
at him then, but she didn't want to chance him hurting
Troy. She hoped the small gun didn't fall out as she was
tied up and then pushed into the back of a van.

"Troy, what was that all about?" she asked.

"Shh, they have ears everywhere," he said. He scooted his body closer to hers and then leaned down and
whispered in her ear, "You trusting me at this point will
be very important."

"I do." Savannah forgot to whisper.

Savannah had to strain her ear to hear because Troy
was talking so low. "I got something from my couch.
We're both protected."

She knew what he meant. She felt better knowing
that.

Troy continued, saying, "I'm going to do my best to
keep us together, but if by chance we get separated, do
what you have to do. Do not, and I repeat do not, hesitate to kill."

A chill went up Savannah's spine. She would do
whatever she had to do to survive. Troy didn't even
have to tell her that.

"Come here. I need you," Troy said. She leaned her
body into his. Although his arms were tied, it felt as if
he were holding her tight.

The van seemed to hit every bump in the road. Savannah's heart fluttered when she realized the van had
stopped. Troy whispered, "We're about thirty minutes
away from my house."

Savannah wondered how he could do that. He was good, and that was the assurance she would hold on to. She would hold on to that fact as they prepared to go meet the man who could have possibly killed her father. She sat up and scooted back to the other side of the van.

Instead of the goon opening the door, another man, with spiked blond hair, opened the door. "Come on, you two," he said as he dragged Savannah out by her feet.

Savannah almost slipped as her feet hit the concrete. She looked at her surroundings. Nothing looked familiar. They were out in some remote place. She could see nothing but trees and a forest. The road leading to where they were wasn't even a blacktop road. Instead, it was a dusty red. Troy said they were about thirty minutes away from his place, but it had to have been in the opposite direction of where she was used to driving, because none of this looked familiar.

Troy was pulled out next. The guy was rough on him, and she wanted to pop him for hitting Troy on the back of the neck. The goon was standing on the other side of the van. "Follow me."

The goon was in front while the blond-haired man walked behind Troy. The goon entered a code. Savannah made a mental note of it as he opened the door, which sounded more like a vault opening than a door to a building.

She followed him in. Savannah scanned the place and tried to memorize their location as she followed the goon from room to room. "This will be your home away from home," he said as he untied her arms and pushed Savannah into the room. Troy was behind her, but instead of Troy being placed there too, he was pushed back and then the door was closed. She could hear the lock turning.

The room was spacious, but when she heard the clicking sound of the door locking, she began to have a panic attack. "Breathe in and out. In and out," she spoke aloud as she followed her own directions.

"When they open the door, I will be prepared," she told herself.

The room they placed her in had a television and a chair. She plopped in the chair and closed her eyes and prayed. She hoped that Montana and Asia were safe. She prayed that nothing would happen to Troy.

37

Troy wanted to scream "no" when they pushed Savannah into that room by herself. He knew she was probably scared. It was his fault. He should have shot the intruder when he had the chance. But no, he had to get to the bottom of things. He wouldn't be able to live with himself if his error in judgment got Savannah killed.

The memory of her giving all of herself to him the night before made him teary-eyed. He would not let these men take that away from him. It took him years to reconnect with Savannah, and no one would separate them ever again. Not like this. Not now. Not ever.

Troy was pushed into an empty, dark room.

The goon said, "Someone will be with you shortly." The goon laughed as he shut the door on him.

Troy hit the wall and let out a few obscenities. He knew there were cameras watching. He wanted them to think he was out of control. He slid down on the floor for further effect. He closed his eyes and leaned back. He recalled the schematics of what he had seen of the place. The people who brought him here weren't aware that he knew the layout of the building and the grounds, because he was one of the ones who helped pick out the layout. It was set up exactly like the one he used for his security firm.

He hated playing the waiting game, but he had come too far not to find out who had been trying to kill him.

Raymond was the obvious choice, but sometimes things aren't what they seem, so he didn't want to leave anything to chance. He had brought down too many guys. It could be someone from his past who realized where he was, or it could be Raymond. Whoever it was would be in for the surprise of his life.

These men weren't trained properly, because if it had been Troy, he would have done a thorough search; neither seemed to have thought about it. They were trained, but not trained well enough. That was to his advantage.

His body was his timer. He waited and waited. He hoped Savannah wasn't stressing too much. He had noticed they put her in a comfortable-looking room. He was confident in knowing that Savannah was more than capable of handling herself. At least in his heart she was. He didn't want to think otherwise.

Time sped by. According to his body clock, it had now been six hours later. He figured they were waiting on nightfall to hit. This was perfect, because that would make it easier for him and for Savannah to escape. He knew he would need to be fully energized, so he decided to take a nap and wait it out. He'd wait until his captors came to retrieve him.

His eyes popped open as soon as he heard the lock click, but he pretended to be asleep.

"Look at him. To think he was part of The Agency," the goon said.

The guard nudged his arm with the baton. "Wake up. It's teatime."

Troy opened his eyes and appeared to be disoriented.

"Wake up, I said," the goon ordered.

Troy stood up. The bright light beaming in from the hallway temporarily blinded him. He got a quick view of the man's watch. It was eight at night.

"Where's the lady?" he asked.

"Minding her own business," the goon responded.

He would be the second person he knocked out.

Troy was pushed down the hall. The room he was placed in was set up as an interrogation room. He was brought something to drink and eat. He refused to drink or eat because he didn't know if the items had been sabotaged with drugs. He had survived a whole week without drinking or eating, and if he had to do it again, then he would. He hoped it didn't come to that, because Savannah wasn't equipped for that kind of treatment.

The goon came back in the room. "See you weren't hungry. That might be your last supper, so I would have eaten it if I were you."

"But you're not me," Troy responded.

"Come on. The boss is ready for you," the goon said.

Troy followed him out of the room. He was led into what appeared to be an office. No one was in the room except for him at this point. His eyes scanned the room. He saw the security cameras. His eyes zoomed in on the room where Savannah was. She was sitting in a chair curled up. He automatically clenched his fists. "I'm going to get us out of this," Troy said.

"So we meet again," the familiar voice said.

Troy was surprised to see Irene when he turned around. "How did you?"

"Everybody has a price, dear. Even you," she said as she used the cane she was holding and let it trace his face and the left side of his body.

Troy was livid. One of his men had violated his trust. When he got out of this, he would be doing some house cleaning. He played along with her to learn what he needed to know. "Was it Mack? No, it had to be Yasi."

"If you knew Mack was susceptible to bribes, why did you trust him?" She shook her head. "You're slacking, Bridges."

"You're something else, you know that," Troy said as he watched her walk with her cane and sit down. She made sure the split of the long white skirt she was wearing exposed her long, muscular legs.

"All of this could have been yours. Can still be, if you act right," she said. She patted the space next to her. "Come. Sit."

Troy obeyed her. "What do you want, Irene?"

"You. It's always been you."

"I'm not an option."

She looked at the monitor. "You would rather be with Miss Boring, when you could have all of this. What does she have that I don't?"

Troy was about to answer, when Irene said, "Don't. She's not the one for you."

Troy laughed. "Your time in lockup must have dissolved some of your brain cells."

"Just the opposite. Oh, Raymond told me to tell you . . . you should have taken him up on his offer."

"So Raymond's behind all of this?" Troy asked.

"Of course your little friend doesn't know it, but he's the one who killed her father. Major was going to expose all of us. We couldn't have that, could we?"

Troy was thinking of a way to escape. "Raymond and Major were friends. I don't believe you."

Irene leaned her head back and laughed. "In this game nobody's your friend. It's every man"—she laughed—"and woman for themselves. You've played it long enough to know that."

"It's still hard for me to believe. How and why?" Troy asked.

The smile on Irene's face left. "Excuse me, but this isn't twenty questions. It's not about Raymond right now; it's all about me. And you chose another woman over me, so she'll pay for that."

"You better not harm a hair on her body," Troy stated.

"Too bad you won't be around too much longer to find out," Irene said.

"Well, maybe we can work something out," Troy suggested.

"I knew you would see things my way."

Troy stood up. He started unzipping his pants. "Is this what you want?"

Irene's face showed she was surprised. She fanned herself. "Come to Mama."

Troy leaned on her; then instead of kissing her, he hugged her. She moaned. He used his fingers and touched the pressure points on her neck, knocking her out. "One down, and more to go," Troy said.

~ *38* ~

Savannah dreamed Troy was whispering in her ear. She opened her eyes and almost shouted when she realized Troy was there in the flesh and whispering in her ear. She grabbed him and hugged him tight.

"Look, we don't have much time," he said. "Come on."

She followed behind him. The house was dark, so it took Savannah's eyes a minute to adjust. Thankfully, Troy had her by the hand, or they would have gotten separated.

Troy held up his hand to alert her to stop. He pointed to the hallway. She moved back down the hallway. Troy opened up the door that led to another door. He tried to open it, but it wouldn't budge. He ran and used his shoulder to get it to open.

The alarms went off. "Grab as much gear as you can," Troy said as he placed ammunition in his pockets.

Savannah picked up ammunition. "What are these?" Savannah asked.

"These are for night vision. Put one on. Hand me that one," he said.

Savannah did as instructed. "Looks like we hit pay dirt."

"Come on," Troy said.

In her peripheral vision Savannah saw the guard coming. She shouted, "Duck."

She turned just in time to shoot the guard before he could shoot Troy. In a voice barely above a whisper, Troy said, "Baby, you saved my life."

Savannah let out a few deep breaths. "I guess this is how Bonnie felt when she was backing up Clyde."

"Only you would find something to joke about at a time like this," Troy responded. He shot the lock off the door that led to the outside. "Come on, let's get out of here."

The room filled with smoke. "I can't breathe!" Savannah yelled.

"Don't let go of my hand," Troy said.

Savannah held on for dear life. The smoke was blinding her. She knew when they had made it to the outside, because the clean air filled her nostrils. She coughed a few times.

"Get down," Troy said.

She crawled, following Troy. She was so glad for the night vision glasses, because otherwise she would be blind out here in the dark.

"Run, Vanna. Don't look back. Run!" Troy screamed.

Gunshots could be heard coming from behind them. Troy got up and she was not too far behind him. She ran as fast as she could. God had to have been watching out for them, because it was a wonder that none of the bullets reached them.

They were running deeper and deeper into the forest. Under normal circumstances Savannah would have been scared out in the forest at night. She couldn't stand creepy things and was afraid of bears, wolves, and anything slimy. But she would rather be with the beasts of the wild than be locked up in the place from where they had just escaped.

She didn't have time to think about too much because Troy had them running. "Are you okay?" He stopped and asked her this a few times.

"I'm fine," she would respond each time, although she was getting out of breath. If she got out of this, she would increase her workout from three times a week to at least five times a week.

"Let's stop and rest for a minute," Troy said.

"No, I'm fine. We don't have to," Savannah said as she stopped and bent down.

"Vanna, come here," Troy said. He held her in his arms.

Savannah wanted to fall over, but they had come too far for her to give up. "I'm scared, Troy. What if—"

"No what-ifs. You have two sisters at home and it's my duty to get you back to them," Troy said.

She saw him smile, and his million-dollar smile was all she needed to see. "What are you waiting for?" She walked ahead of him.

"Slow down, Annie Oakley," he joked.

She followed him into what looked like a cave. "Troy, why are we stopping? I thought we needed to keep going."

"I don't hear anyone coming behind us, so that means they are waiting for daylight. We'll rest here for a while and then get started again," he responded.

Savannah could hear what sounded like crickets. She heard a howl, which sent a chill up her spine. Before she realized it, she was reaching for Troy. If he hadn't caught her, she would have fallen.

"Sorry," she said.

"Come over here," Troy said as he cleared off a spot for her to sit down.

"Ouch," she said as she removed the stem that she sat on. "This night air is a little chilly."

Troy wrapped his arms around her. "Vanna, I'm sorry."

"For what?" she wondered.

"All of this could have been avoided if I would have let you shoot the guy when he was back at the house."

"Hey, I thought you had a good idea. I wanted to see who the boss man was as well."

He brushed the grass out of her hair and said, "I did find out some things."

Savannah halfway listened to him give her a recap of the conversation he had with Irene. Her mind was still spinning from what Irene said about Raymond being behind her father's death. First she had to get out of her current situation. She asked, "Do you really think we can get out of this?"

"Baby, you're with me. I'm the king." He playfully hit himself on his chest.

Savannah leaned her head back on his chest. "Well, just get your queen to safety and she'll be highly appreciative."

Savannah didn't know when she dozed off. Troy's hand brushing gently across her face woke her up. He whispered in her ear, "We're not alone."

"But—"

"Shh," he said. "Ease up."

Savannah got up as quietly as she could. She could hear her heart beat. She could feel Troy's breath on the nape of her neck.

Troy held up two fingers. She realized he meant two people. He pointed at himself and then in the opposite direction. He pointed at Savannah and then in the opposite direction of her. Savannah followed his lead. She went one way, while he went the other. They backtracked and were able to sneak up on the intruders.

Troy grabbed one of the intruders around the neck. He reached for his gun. The gun fired before it fell to the ground. Savannah didn't hesitate to shoot the other intruder before he could react. He fell to the ground. Neither man was dead, but they wouldn't be coming after them either.

Troy went through their pockets. He found a pair of handcuffs and handcuffed them together. Savannah found a cell phone in the other intruder's pocket. She attempted to dial a number, but the call wouldn't go through. "Dang it!" she yelled.

"Grab his weapon," Troy stated.

Savannah placed the cell phone in her bra, because her pockets were full. She followed Troy deeper into the woods, or so she thought.

~ 39~

Troy hoped his memory was correct. They had walked deep into the woods, and there was a road on the opposite side. Getting onto the road wouldn't guarantee their safety, but it could get them back to the highway. Once they were at the highway, he knew he could hitch them a ride to safety.

His throat was dry. He needed some water bad. "Are you okay?" he asked Savannah.

"Yes," she said as she walked beside him through the brush. "Uh, Troy. I think I stepped on something."

He looked down. "Don't panic."

"Uh. What is it?" she said between clenched teeth.

"It was only the remains of a small animal."

Savannah began shaking her foot and jumping around. "Ugh. Get it off. Get if off."

Troy picked up a stick from the ground and held her foot and wiped as much as he could off.

"Thank you," Savannah said.

If they weren't running for their lives, Savannah's little antics would have been comical. He would file this scene away for future reference. Maybe one day when they were alone in bed reminiscing about their lives, years later, they could both look back at this and laugh.

Troy saw the headlights. "Come on. Let's stay on the edge."

They walked closer toward the road. Savannah said, "Did you see that?"

"Yes. But we can't be sure if they are friend or foe . . . so keep it moving," he said.

Troy was relieved to see a pond. He practically dragged Savannah near there. He bent down and cupped the water in his hands. He didn't care how it tasted; he just needed to wet his taste buds. "You better drink something," Troy said.

Savannah didn't move. "I'll pass."

Troy splashed some water on her face. "Come on, it's not all bad."

"No."

Troy knew Savannah was stubborn. He hoped he was able to get them to safety, because he hated for her to pass out from dehydration. Savannah leaned down and splashed water on her face. She licked her tongue out. "If I do it like this, it's not so bad."

He laughed. "I love you, girl."

In between splashes, she said, "And I love you too."

Troy's ears pricked up. He thought he heard some dogs barking. "That's enough. Let's move on."

He grabbed Savannah's arm and increased their pace. He saw some lights approaching from the road. They had to take their chances. The barking was getting louder, and he wasn't sure of how many men and dogs were close on their trail.

"Baby, this is the deal. We're going to flag down the passerby. If they stop, let me do all of the talking. If they don't cooperate, we'll have to use force."

"That's criminal."

"No, it's surviving," he responded.

They removed their night vision goggles and placed the guns in their pocket. They flagged down the motorist. The car almost hit them and screeched to the side of the road.

A young couple exited the car. "Are you all right?" the woman said.

"We're fine. Our car broke down. We need your help," Troy said.

The young man said, "Sure. We can drop you off at the next exit. We need to stop and get some gas, anyway. Come on, get in."

Troy heard the dogs getting louder and louder. "Thanks." He hoped they would hurry. The young man liked to talk. Troy wanted him to drive. "We appreciate the ride," Troy said.

"No problem. We're headed out of town, or else we would still be in bed."

Troy patted his foot. He saw the apprehension on Savannah's face.

Savannah said, "Where to?"

The young lady spoke. "We're headed to Savannah, Georgia."

"Really. My name's Savannah," she volunteered.

"Cool. Must be Kismet," she said.

"Totally, dude," the young man responded.

"My cell phone's not working. Do either one of you happen to have one?" Savannah asked.

The young lady turned around and handed her one.

When they passed the entranceway to where they just escaped, Troy noticed the place was lit up. More cars were there than when they had first arrived.

"Let me see that," Troy said. He dialed Cheryl's number.

"Where's that gas station?" he asked the young man.

"It's the Busy Bee on Plank Road," he responded.

Troy said, "Have them meet me at the Busy Bee on Beltline Road. Pronto." He handed the cell phone back to the kind young woman.

The parking lot was well lit when they pulled up into the gas station, which was also a restaurant and truck stop.

"Thank you. I lost my wallet out in the woods," Troy lied.

"No problem. Do a good deed and it'll come back to you. That's what my papa always says," the young man said.

"It was nice meeting you," Savannah said to the young woman.

"Same here," she responded.

"You two be safe now," Troy said.

"We will, mister. Thank you for the company."

Troy and Savannah didn't realize how rough they looked until they saw their reflection in the mirror in the gas station. Troy said, "Come on. I don't think we should sit still long. We need to get us another ride out of here. We don't have time to wait on my people. I have a feeling they are fast on our trail."

Savannah used her assets to get one of the truck drivers to give them a ride into the city. "Now, I normally don't pick up hitchhikers, but you two. Something tells me you're not your average hitchhikers," the older gentleman said.

Troy said, "Sir, we do appreciate it."

Troy didn't think anything of it until he realized they were headed in the opposite direction of the city. He didn't want to crash, but they were headed back toward the compound. He refused to let that happen. Troy removed the gun from his pocket and held it up to the driver's head. "Stop this truck now."

"Troy, what are you doing?" Savannah yelled from the backseat of the trailer.

The truck driver ignored Troy's command. Troy clicked back the revolver. "Buckle up, baby. I'm only going to give you three seconds, and if you don't stop this rig now, all of us are going to be closer to meeting our Maker. One . . . two . . ." Troy was about to let the gun go off when the driver stopped.

"A call went on the CB radio about you two. A reward was offered. You two fit the bill. I didn't mean no harm."

Troy popped him upside the head; then he reached over, opened the door, and pushed him out. He closed the door and remained behind the wheel.

40

Savannah jumped in the seat that Troy had occupied earlier. "You know how to drive this thing."

"Watch me," he said as he put the truck in gear. Fortunately, there was not a trailer hooked up to it, so Troy was able to back up and maneuver it and turned the truck around. He pulled the horn. He looked at Savannah. "I always wanted to do that."

She laughed. Troy turned on the CB radio. Savannah said, "Uh, I think you need to keep your eyes on the road."

"I got this," he joked.

She pulled the phone out of her bosom. There was still no signal. She threw the phone to the back and said, "That piece of junk."

Troy handed her a phone that was hooked up to a charger. "Try this."

"Four bars!" Savannah said.

Troy would have sworn she was doing a cell phone commercial from the excitement she portrayed for seeing the cell phone with four bars on the display screen instead of none.

Savannah dialed Asia's cell phone number. "Voice mail. Go figure." She hung up and dialed her home number. Still, no answer. "Dang it. You got to get me home."

"First we need to dump this truck," Troy said.

Savannah leaned back and let her hair blow in the wind. She tried her best to keep the hair from falling in her face. The last few days had been rough. She prayed for Montana and Asia's safety. The phone rang, breaking her from her trance. She looked at the display and saw Asia's number. "Girl, where are you guys?"

Asia responded, "We're at Montana's. Her place is the only place no one has broken into, so we decided to camp out here. Where are you? Did Troy kidnap you?"

"If you only knew," Savannah responded. "Look, don't go back to my place. I'll meet you at Montana's."

"Sis, you don't sound too good."

"I'm fine. Just fine," Savannah said. Now that she knew they were okay, she could relax.

Troy pulled the truck into a parking lot. "Baby, we got to go," he said.

"Asia, I'll see you later." Savannah hung up the phone. She was about to put it back in the cradle, but she thought better of it and kept it.

When she got down from the truck, Troy was talking to a few familiar faces. She recalled seeing them during their training at Troy's facility. She was so relieved to see them. She wanted to jump up and down for joy.

Savannah got into the backseat of one of the SUVs as they were driven to Troy's office. Troy handed her a bag. "There are some women's clothes in there. The shower is that way."

Savannah wasn't too sure about showering with a load of men out there. Troy must have sensed her hesitation, because he said, "I'll be right outside the door. Nobody's going to bother you. These are the good guys."

The water hitting her body massaged not only her body but her soul. Each hot drop of water helped release the tension that had built up in the last twenty-four hours. She washed the dirt out of her hair. She dried off and looked at her reflection. Once she exited the bathroom, she went to Troy's receptionist desk and found a couple of rubber bands. She pulled her hair back in a ponytail. Her hair was slick, black, and wet. It would fluff up when it air-dried. Troy was sitting at the head of the table when she entered the room. Everyone stood up to offer a seat to her.

"No. Sit. I'll sit here," she said, grabbing a chair at the other end of the table.

She listened as Troy went over everything that had happened to them. She felt like she was living someone else's life. Everything up until this point had been surreal. She wanted it all to be over with so she could go back to living a normal life. Who was she fooling? Her life hadn't been normal since her dad died. She didn't realize when she set out to find his killer that she would be fighting for her life, fighting for the safety of her sisters. She had to ask herself if it was all worth it. A part of her said no, but the part that wanted to avenge her dad's death knew that she would do it all again, minus the part where Montana got hurt. If she could do it again, she would send her sisters far away, so whoever was guilty would only have her to target.

After Troy finished talking to his team, they dispersed. He walked to the other end of the table and sat on the edge. He reached for her hands. He held them up and kissed them. "I'm a lucky man."

"Where is all of this coming from?"

"I was watching you a while ago and it dawned on me how much you care," Troy said.

Savannah smiled. "You've done so much for me. For my sisters."

"I don't deserve you," Troy said.

"Don't ever say that."

"I thought I was going to lose you. I can do without a lot of things, but not you. Baby, I don't know what I would do if I lost you."

Savannah stood up. She kissed him. They held each other like that, until they heard someone clear his throat.

"Don't mean to interrupt," Mike said.

Savannah moved from in between Troy's legs. Troy stood up from the table. "Did you find our abductor?" Troy asked.

"He was DOA."

"Dang it. He took the easy route."

"Troy, don't worry. We'll do a clean sweep. If he wasn't the only one, I'll find out soon enough."

Cheryl rushed in. "Irene's dead too. Our guys got to the compound, and when the dust settled, most of their men were down."

Savannah watched them in motion.

"Any of our men hurt?" Troy asked. Savannah could hear the concern in his voice.

"A few got shot, but no casualties," Cheryl responded.

Savannah saw Troy's chest fall and rise during the course of their conversation.

"Do you need anything else, Ms. Savannah?" Cheryl asked.

"Cheryl, when you say my name like that, it makes me seem so old." She laughed. "No, I'm fine."

Troy said, "We're about to head out. I'm taking her to her sisters, or else she's going to kill me."

Thirty minutes later, Savannah was hugging Montana and Asia.

"Girl, you look a hot mess," Asia commented.

"And I love you too," Savannah responded.

"Hi, Troy," Montana said. "We didn't mean to ignore you, but you know how we can be."

"I don't mind at all. Seeing women hug like that is a man's fantasy."

Savannah popped him on the arm. "You're so nasty."

"You should know," Troy said as he left the room.

Asia said, "Ooh, you didn't!"

Savannah ignored her. "There's more to life than sex, like the fact that I was kidnapped."

"What? When were you going to tell us?" Montana and Asia blurted out question after question.

41

Troy watched the exchange between the sisters. He loved Savannah's sisters as if they were his sisters. After he was sure Montana's place was secure, he sat on the sofa next to Savannah. He placed his arm around her as if it was always meant to be there.

"I'm jealous. Where's my knight in shining armor?" Asia joked.

"I have a friend," Troy said.

Montana held her hand up to protest. "No. The last friend you introduced us to was a little on the crazy side."

"He definitely rode the short bus to school." Asia used her hand to make a horn motion. "Toot. Toot."

"I did apologize," Troy said.

"We forgive you, but that's okay. We'll find our own men," Montana stated.

Asia said, "So, are you two officially a couple?"

Savannah spoke before Troy could say anything. "You all have a bad habit of talking about me as if I'm not here."

"Well, are you?" Montana said while she crossed her arms.

Savannah looked at Troy. Troy shrugged his shoulders. "I'm all hers, if she'll have me."

"I'll think about it," Savannah responded. Troy looked at her with a boyish grin. He batted his eyes. "Okay. Yes, we're a couple."

Troy kissed her and didn't care that she would probably slap him for doing so, because her sisters were around. To his surprise she didn't. In fact, she got all into it.

Asia cleared her throat. "My virgin eyes."

Savannah stopped kissing Troy. She threw a pillow at Asia. "Please. You haven't been a virgin since—"

"Vanna!" Asia screamed.

"Okay. I wouldn't want my new boyfriend to think one of my sisters is a slush puppy."

Troy's new cell phone vibrated. "I need to get this," he said.

He walked to another room and talked to Mike. He went over his plan to trap Raymond. Raymond had tried to kill him too many times. He could not go without being punished. The local police were not going to be able to detain Raymond. His security clearance was too high up on the chain. In order to stop Raymond Steel, Troy would have to beat him at his own game. It was time for Raymond to be the hunted. He watched the Blake sisters' easy banter with one another. He needed them to trap Raymond. Would they go for the plan? He hoped so. He hoped Savannah would forgive him this one last time.

"Ladies, I don't mean to interrupt, but I needed to talk to you about something," he said. Instead of sitting by Savannah, Troy stood up so he could see each of their facial expressions when he went over his plan.

"Irene confirmed verbally that Raymond is behind my attacks. But what I didn't tell Savannah, because I needed her to concentrate on getting to safety, is Irene also confirmed that Raymond killed your dad."

"That bastard. A part of me believed Vanna was making it all up," Montana said.

Savannah's face turned red. "I'll kill him. I'll kill him with my bare hands."

Troy tried to calm them down. "No. We're going to get him, but this is where you three come in. I need you to lure him over to Savannah's place."

"I don't know about that. I won't be held accountable for what I'll do if I lay eyes on him again," Asia stated. The pillow in her hands was twisted. She threw it on the floor.

"This is the plan," Troy said as he told them what each one of their roles would be. He already had a team of people setting things up at Savannah's.

Savannah crossed her legs. "So I'm supposed to act like I hate you now."

"Exactly. You have to say some things to make it believable."

"Like how ever since we met, my life has been in danger."

"Ouch," Troy responded.

"I think it's a stupid idea, and I don't want to have anything to do with it. If it puts Montana and Asia in the line of fire, my response is no. Find another way." Savannah stormed out of the room.

Montana said, "I think it's a good idea."

"Me too," Asia added. "But it's Savannah you need to convince."

Troy left Asia and Montana in the living room. Savannah was out on the patio; she was gazing up at the stars. He watched her before approaching her. He attempted to touch her shoulder but was thrown off when her first reaction was to jerk back.

She turned around and faced him. "How dare you? After all I've gone through. I told you I didn't want my sisters in danger."

"They won't be. My men are situated there. If he tries anything, he's as good as dead."

"You don't get it, do you? Those two practically idol-ized him, especially Montana. She's not going to admit it, but this ordeal with Raymond is hurting her more than she's letting on. Yes, I'm hurt and disappointed, but I'm older. For some reason Montana was his favor-ite," Savannah blurted out.

"Have I ever led you wrong?"

Savannah glared at him.

"Okay, let me rephrase that. If we don't do this now, if we don't try to get him to confess, he's not going to stop. He's not going to rest until he's sure that no one—you and I, your sisters—can tell the authorities of his crooked way of doing things. Believe me, there are some people who are going to agree with him. How-ever, there are those people, like you and your sisters, and, yes, even me, who know that killing people—just for the sake of killing them—isn't right . . . even when those people are known murderers."

Savannah reached out to him. Troy pulled her into his arms. He ran his hand over her thick ponytail. She said, "I'm scared. I'm scared of what I might do. I don't know if I can control myself. I might pull out my gun and shoot him right on the spot. What if I can't control myself? What if I can't control getting revenge on my daddy's killer?" Savannah said in between sobs.

Troy moved back so they could look in each other's faces. "Look at me." Savannah wouldn't. "Look at me. You're not like him. You're going to do the right thing. You're going to talk to him. You're going to use your skills to talk him into confessing. I have a one hundred percent . . . correction. I have two hundred percent confidence that you can get him to confess."

Troy moved away. His arms went up in the air. "Do you honestly think I would have you do this if I thought you couldn't do it? If I were like him, he would be dead right now. I could have had one of my men take him out, and he never would have known a thing. See, Raymond thinks he's smart, but he's the type of guy who has other people do his dirty work. Because guess what? He's not that good. He's only good at giving orders, not executing them himself. You and I. We're good. Any other woman would have cracked under the pressure you've been under, but you, girl, you're a champ. Major taught you well. He would be proud."

Savannah pulled Troy back into her arms. "I'm a lucky girl."

Troy kissed her forehead. "No, I'm the lucky one."

"If you ever get tired of doing what you do, you could have a career in speech writing. That was a lovely speech," Savannah teased.

"You should be a comedienne in your second life, because you're incredibly funny." Troy then added, "And oh so sexy."

"One of us should be able to tell a joke, because, mister, your jokes are lame," Savannah said.

"I resemble that remark." Troy laughed.

Savannah didn't. "See? That was corny."

By now, they had returned to the living room. Savannah faced her sisters. "It's a go."

Asia stood up first. "Let's do this."

~ *42* ~

It didn't take much to convince Raymond to meet her at her place. He was actually shocked to hear from her. He continued to play the role of the concerned uncle. Troy rode with them in Asia's car, just in case someone was watching them and recognized his other vehicle.

Savannah was amazed that she didn't know anyone had been in her place. She was a stickler about things, and nothing seemed to be out of place. "Your people are good," she told Troy.

"I only hire the best," he responded.

"So what now?" Asia asked.

"You all go about doing things as normal. I'll make myself scarce. I'll be upstairs if you need me," Troy said.

Savannah followed him up the stairs. She pushed him into her room and closed the door. She locked her lips so quickly around his mouth, Troy didn't even know how to react. He allowed her to have her way with his mouth. She devoured each moan.

"I want you so bad," Troy said in between their kisses.

By now, they were near the bed. Savannah pushed him on the bed and lay on top of him as their bodies ground together. The adrenaline rush was sending them both over the edge. The sound of the doorbell broke the trance.

"Showtime," Savannah said as she stood up and brushed herself off. She winked at Troy and left him lying across the bed on his back.

"Uncle Raymond, I'm so glad you could come," Savannah said as she hugged him.

"You girls mean the world to me. I told you to call me if you need me."

Savannah grabbed his hand and led him into the living room, where Asia and Montana sat. They acknowledged him but didn't show the same amount of affection as Savannah had.

"Well, I don't know where to begin," Savannah said as she sat in the chair across from him.

"I got time," he said, looking at his watch.

She looked at Montana and then at Asia. "We owe you an apology. I owe you an apology."

"Baby girl, I would have—"

"No . . . let me finish. You tried to warn me. Warn *us* about Troy. Do you know that Troy almost got me killed? If I hadn't gotten out when I did, you wouldn't be talking to me right now," Savannah insisted.

Raymond balled up his fist. "I'll handle Troy. You just leave him to me."

"I trusted him. He even tried to turn us against you. I don't know how I could have believed the lies coming out of his mouth. Will you ever forgive me? Us?" Savannah asked.

"This has been hard on you all. I don't hold anything against any of you. Let me handle Bridges. He'll no longer be a problem after tonight."

"This little reunion has been nice, but I have to get to work tomorrow," Asia said.

Montana stood up. "Me too. Love you, Uncle Raymond."

Savannah watched them each hug him.

"You girls be safe now. Don't worry about a thing, you hear me," he said.

"We won't." Asia winked before walking away.

A few seconds later, Savannah heard the front door close. Part one of the plan had worked. Now that she was alone with him, it was now on to part two. The house phone rang. She picked it up. She said, "Uh-huh. Are you sure? . . . No. I don't believe you. . . Look, until you can get me some concrete proof . . . lose my number. . . In fact . . . don't call me. I'll call you."

Savannah turned back around to face Raymond. "That was a crank caller."

"Now, Vanna, I can tell when you're lying," he said.

"You got me. That was Troy. He's such a pest."

"Like unwanted pests, he will be eliminated," Raymond responded.

Savannah's smile faded. "Now that we're alone, there's something I want to ask you."

Raymond leaned back and crossed his leg. "I'm all yours." He looked at his watch. "Well, for at least the next thirty minutes."

Savannah sat across from him. "It won't take that long," she promised. "Troy's a liar. That's been established, right?"

"Right."

"I've been thinking. The day I found Dad, there was no sign of an intruder. In fact, the door was locked. Whoever killed him had to have known him, because there was no way he would have gone out without a fight. I read the police report several times, and there was no mention of a struggle."

Raymond uncrossed his leg and sat up. "Baby girl, I don't know if I like where you're going with this conversation."

Savannah leaned forward. "You might not. But hear me out. Dad didn't have too many friends. You were the only one besides the neighbors that I knew of, and I know the neighbors didn't do it."

"Are you accusing me of killing Major?"

"You said it, I didn't," Savannah responded.

Raymond stood up. "My patience is thin, so I better leave."

Savannah ran and blocked his way. "No, you're going to look me in the face and tell me you did not murder my father."

Raymond pushed her out of the way. Savannah almost stumbled and fell. He reached to help her up. "Don't. Don't touch me ever again!" she shouted.

"Look, this conversation is going nowhere. You want to know what happened. Do you really want to know what happened?" he said as he pulled out a weapon.

Savannah was startled. She backed up and ended up falling back on the couch. She turned her body to face Raymond. A chill crept up her spine as she stared into a set of darkened eyes that revealed more than words.

His tone confirmed he was no longer pretending to be nice Uncle Raymond. "You couldn't leave it alone, could you? Montana and Asia have not only lost their father, but they're about to lose an older sister."

Savannah shouted, "You bastard! We trusted you. How could you? You knew he was all we had. He wouldn't have turned you in, and you know it. He loved you like a brother, and this is how you betrayed him."

"Betrayal? Major betrayed me in the worst way. I was the one who recommended him to The Agency, and he had the nerve to question me. *Me*." He looked around as if he had an audience. "If it hadn't been for me, The Agency would be just another useless agency that the government is funding. See, Major's problem is he had little dreams. Me, I want it all. How do you think I'm able to live in the neighborhood I live in? Not from the money the government pays, that's for sure. Major couldn't understand that. I tried to cut him in on the deals many times, but he wouldn't have it."

"My dad was an honorable man. Something I wish I could say about you, but can't," Savannah blurted out.

"You're your father's daughter. Like him, you went snooping around. He wouldn't stop until he had solid evidence, he told me. I mean, how bold can you be? He thought he was untouchable. He thought our ties were enough to protect him. But he was wrong."

Savannah said, "The Agency's motto is to serve and protect citizens from terrorists and anyone who means people in this nation harm. It did not say serve, protect, and kill people you deemed guilty."

"You know nothing about how it is out there. My men risk their lives every single day and night, while the rest of you go around as if life should be served to you on a silver platter."

"Raymond, you are crazy, and if I have to go to the president myself, I will make sure they get that disc."

Raymond laughed. "You forgot. You gave me the disc. Besides, who is going to listen to a dead woman?"

Raymond aimed the gun at Savannah. Savannah, without flinching, used one of her legs and swung it up. Her movement caught him by surprise as her foot made contact with his hand and knocked the gun out of it.

Raymond darted for the gun, but Troy knocked him out before he could reach it.

The front door swung open and in walked other law enforcement agents. Asia and Montana ran in behind them. They headed straight for Savannah.

"We heard everything," Montana said. "How could I have been so stupid?"

"He had us all fooled," Savannah said as she hugged them both. "I'll be right back. I need to go say something to my hero."

"Go get him, girl," Asia said.

Savannah waited for Troy to finish speaking with the agent. "Ma'am, we need to get your statement too."

Savannah told him everything that had happened. Troy handed them a disc. "This is what all of this was about," Troy said.

The agent placed it in an evidence bag. "Prisoners don't take too kindly to former law enforcement behind bars."

"That's what I'm counting on," Savannah said.

"We'll be in contact. You and your sisters might be called to the witness stand when this thing goes to trial."

"I look forward to that day," Savannah responded.

Savannah allowed Troy to handle things while she and her sisters stood in the background, observing. A few hours later the place was empty. Savannah closed the door and locked it. She leaned on the door and let out a sigh of relief.

"It's over. It's finally over!" she yelled. She stood in the living-room doorway. Troy was drinking some water. Montana had the TV remote and was flipping from station to station. Mike was still around. Asia and Mike were debating.

"Seems like old times," Savannah said.

"I can't wait to sleep in my own bed again," Asia commented.

"Mike, go with her. Make sure it's still safe, will you?" Troy said.

"I can take care of myself. Only thing Mike would do is get in the way, anyway," she responded.

"Man, you're going to let her talk to you like that?" Troy asked.

"Did she say something? I thought it was a bunch of hot air," Mike teased.

They argued all the way out the door.

Troy looked at Savannah and said, "They'll be okay. Well, if Asia doesn't kill him first."

They laughed. "Montana, you can stay over if you want."

Montana threw the remote on the couch and stood up. "Oh no, I'm not going to be a third wheel in this party. I'm going home."

Montana walked out the door and then turned back around. "Vanna, can I borrow your car? I forgot Asia drove."

Savannah went to retrieve her keys. "Do not go over the speed limit."

"Yes, big sis," Montana teased. She hugged and kissed her on the cheek.

Savannah watched her pull out of the garage. She hit the button to let the garage down. She bumped into Troy when she turned around. He was holding wineglasses and a bottle of wine.

"I think it's time for a toast," he said.

"I agree." They walked to the kitchen counter and sat on the bar stools. Troy popped the cork and poured two glasses of white wine.

"To my hero," Savannah said as she held up her glass.

"I'll drink to that," Troy said. "Let's see. To the woman who knocked me off my feet, and I mean literally."

They laughed. "I'll drink to that." Then Savannah said, "I got another one. To the Blake sisters."

"To the Blake sisters. Y'all some bad mama jamas," Troy said.

Their glasses clicked again. After drinking a few glasses of wine, Savannah and Troy were tipsy. Not off the wine, but from being in each other's company. "Whoever makes it to the stairs last has to wash the other one's back," Savannah said as she slid from the bar stool and they ran to the stairway. She threw her hands up in the air. "You lose."

Troy turned her around to face him. He kissed her. "No, baby, I'm a winner. Because to wash your back is an honor."

Troy's phone rang. Savannah headed up the stairs. "Don't make me wait too long."

Savannah poured her favorite scent of bubble bath into the steaming water. She retrieved a few towels, because it could get messy. She was glad that she moved into the master bedroom. The bathtub was big enough to fit two. This would be the first time she took a bath with a man in this tub. Actually, it would be the first time she had a bath with any man, anywhere. Period. Troy would be her first.

She felt his presence the moment he came to the door. He didn't say anything. She pretended to be oblivious to him being there. She slowly removed her clothes. When she got down to taking off her panties, she turned around and winked at him.

"You sly thing, you," Troy said as he entered the bathroom.

Savannah entered the bathtub and purposely splashed water on Troy. She blew bubbles at him. She found it sexy to watch him undress. The sight of him in his little boxers turned her on. There wasn't anything little about Troy. The sight of him was enough to make the water temperature go up a notch or two.

They took turns washing each other's bodies. Savannah couldn't remember sharing such an intimate moment with any other man. She had never experienced the feeling she had inside every time Troy touched her body. They were in their own little world. No one else mattered. She picked up the dry towel and wiped the water off Troy's body. Her hand went over every muscle. His body heat radiated onto hers. Troy was the man who broke her lackluster track record with men. He broke Savannah's curse.

About the Author

Shelia M. Goss is the *Essence* magazine and Black Expressions Book Club bestselling author of *My Invisible Husband, Roses Are Thorns (Violets Are True), Paige's Web, Double Platinum, His Invisible Wife, Hollywood Deception, Delilah*, and the Young Adult series *The Lip Gloss Chronicles: The Ultimate Test, Splitsville*, and *Paper Thin*. *Savannah's Curse* is her eleventh novel. Besides writing fiction, she is a freelance writer. She's also the recipient of three *Shades of Romance* Magazine Reader's Choice Multi-Cultural Awards and honored as a Literary Diva: The Top 100 Most Admired African American Women in Literature. To learn more, visit her Web site: www.sheliagoss.com, www.facebook.com/sheliagoss or follow her on twitter at www.twitter.com/sheliamgoss.

Notes

Notes

Notes

ORDER FORM
URBAN BOOKS, LLC
78 E. Industry Ct
Deer Park, NY 11729

Name: (please print): _____

Address: _____

City/State: _____

Zip: _____

QTY	TITLES	PRICE
	16 ½ On The Block	$14.95
	16 On The Block	$14.95
	Betrayal	$14.95
	Both Sides Of The Fence	$14.95
	Cheesecake And Teardrops	$14.95
	Denim Diaries	$14.95
	Happily Ever Now	$14.95
	Hell Has No Fury	$14.95
	If It Isn't love	$14.95
	Last Breath	$14.95
	Loving Dasia	$14.95
	Say It Ain't So	$14.95

Shipping and handling-add $3.50 for 1st book, then $1.75 for each additional book.
Please send a check payable to:
Urban Books, LLC
Please allow 4-6 weeks for delivery

ORDER FORM
URBAN BOOKS, LLC
78 E. Industry Ct
Deer Park, NY 11729

Name: (please print): _____

Address: _____

City/State: _____

Zip: _____

QTY	TITLES	PRICE
	The Cartel	$14.95
	The Cartel 2	$14.95
	The Dopeman's Wife	$14.95
	The Prada Plan	$14.95
	Gunz And Roses	$14.95
	Snow White	$14.95
	A Pimp's Life	$14.95
	Hush	$14.95
	Little Black Girl Lost 1	$14.95
	Little Black Girl Lost 2	$14.95
	Little Black Girl Lost 3	$14.95
	Little Black Girl Lost 4	$14.95

Shipping and handling-add $3.50 for 1st book, then $1.75 for each additional book.

Please send a check payable to:

Urban Books, LLC

Please allow 4-6 weeks for delivery

ORDER FORM
URBAN BOOKS, LLC
78 E. Industry Ct
Deer Park, NY 11729

Name: (please print):_____

Address: _____

City/State: _____

Zip: _____

QTY	TITLES	PRICE
	A Man's Worth	$14.95
	Abundant Rain	$14.95
	Battle Of Jericho	$14.95
	By The Grace Of God	$14.95
	Dance Into Destiny	$14.95
	Divorcing The Devil	$14.95
	Forsaken	$14.95
	Grace And Mercy	$14.95
	Guilty Of Love	$14.95
	His Woman, His Wife, His Widow	$14.95
	Illusions	$14.95
	The LoveChild	$14.95

Shipping and handling-add $3.50 for 1ˢᵗ book, then $1.75 for each additional book.

Please send a check payable to:

Urban Books, LLC

Please allow 4-6 weeks for delivery

ORDER FORM
URBAN BOOKS, LLC
78 E. Industry Ct
. Deer Park, NY 11729

Name:(please print):_____

Address: _____

City/State: _____

Zip: _____

QTY	TITLES	PRICE

Shipping and handling-add $3.50 for 1st book, then $1.75 for each additional book.

Please send a check payable to:
   Urban Books, LLC
Please allow 4-6 weeks for delivery